**IT WASN'T SOMETHING YOU GOT USED TO, FINDING BODIES,** and despite the fact that this was his second one, or maybe because of that fact, Pete found himself unable to accept what he was seeing. The pink sweater that undulated over a trapped bubble of air *could* be a balloon . . .

He whispered at the limp form as he pulled it out of the water, "Bentley?"

He carried her out of the water and laid her down on the sand . . .

It seemed obscene to him as he looked down at the limp form, its youth screaming out at him from every finger, that the seventeen years Bentley Brown had lived were all the years she was ever going to get. He wasn't quite able to believe it. He found himself thinking suddenly of himself at seventeen, looking back at what the years had continued to offer him and would never, now, be offering her . . .

---

Praise for the first
Peter Bartholomew mystery,
*Hot Water*

"An extremely likeable sleuth . . . a dandy mystery puzzle . . ."

— *Library Bulletin*

"Gunning . . . knows her             Entertaining reading."

*Cod Times*

"Sally Gunning bri              of small-town life to her              gettable cast of characters              ck to the next Peter Barthol

—*Mystery News*

**Books by Sally Gunning**

Hot Water
Under Water

Published by POCKET BOOKS

# UNDER WATER

by

## SALLY GUNNING

### A PETER BARTHOLOMEW MYSTERY

**POCKET BOOKS**

New York   London   Toronto   Sydney   Tokyo   Singapore

An *Original* Publication of POCKET BOOKS

POCKET BOOKS, a division of Simon & Schuster Inc.
1230 Avenue of the Americas, New York, NY 10020

ISBN: 0-671-72805-9

First Pocket Books printing February 1992

10  9  8  7  6  5  4  3  2  1

Cover art by Jeffrey Adams

Printed in the U.S.A.

*For Tom,*
*who always gets the jokes,*
*as well as the big picture*

# UNDER WATER

# Chapter
# 1

Peter Bartholomew looked out at the green-gold September marsh, stretched out his stride to keep up with the hopping fifteen-year-old beside him, and ducked just in time to avoid a flailing arm. Maxine Peck was, once again, griping about her mother, and because her mother also happened to be Pete's business partner, Pete was often struggling himself to keep afloat on the turbulent seas of this mother-daughter relationship.

"She's so *embarrassing!*" said Maxine. "I mean she's so *excited* all the time! I mean if she were here, we wouldn't be walking along like this in this nice peace and *quiet!* We'd have to be *enjoying* things! *Noticing* everything! The blue *sky!*" Her right arm sailed high. "The sea *lavender.*" The left arm shot out across Pete's nose. "The stupid old *wa—*" Maxine's right arm had stabbed at the water, but she stopped walking and talking all at once. "Hey!" she hollered. "A balloon!" And just like that the studied ennui of fifteen years of life fell away and the little girl underneath broke into a run, both arms flapping, high-top purple sneakers splashing through the tide pools, over the rocks, and into the lapping waves of the Sound.

Pete smiled, enjoying this brief glimpse of the little girl again—her sixty-two-dollar jeans were sopping wet; her

1

black, spiky hair was flattening out in the wind, and she didn't stop once to fuss with it. Pete approached the edge of the water, still watching the girl, looking down only long enough to guard his own sneakers from the edge of the waves, spying in that one glance a flash of gold through the crystal water. He stooped to pick it up—it was a ring, a heavy gold ring with a blue faceted stone. Pete looked up. Maxine had reached the balloon and was just stooping over it when she stopped at an awkward angle, stiffened, and then snapped up straight. Pete shoved the ring into his pocket and broke into a run; he was already halfway there before Maxine started screaming.

It wasn't something you got used to, finding bodies, and despite the fact that this was his second one, or maybe because of that fact, Pete found himself unable to accept what he was seeing. The pink sweater that undulated over a trapped bubble of air *could* be a balloon, the one eye that popped above the surface and then lolled back under *might* belong to a fish. Pete's last body had been underwater also. Last time he had pulled it out at once, but this time he was more worried about Maxine, who had jammed her still-screaming mouth into his shirt and was clutching his sleeves as if she were the one who was drowning, and it wasn't until he caught what she was screaming that he shoved her away and grabbed hold of the pink sweater and pulled.

"Bentley! It's Bentley! It's Bentley!"

Pete, who had had the misfortune to run into the knife end of a nut at the beginning of the summer and had consequently been in the hospital or otherwise preoccupied for most of the time that the identical twins, Carlisle and Bentley Brown, had been working for him, could still not tell one from the other unless they were standing side by side. He accepted Maxine at her word and whispered at the limp form as he pulled it out of the water, "Bentley?"

There was no answer except for Maxine's wail. Pete turned to her and spoke harshly, in a voice he knew she

2

had never heard from him before, punching out her name to make sure he would attract her attention. "Maxine. Go back to the office. Call the police. Tell them your name and where you are and what you found."

Maxine stared at him.

"*Now*. And say what?"

"Who I am. What I found."

"And where. Tell them where you found her. Now, what will you say?"

"Who I am. Where I found Bentley."

She ran off ahead of him, her run so different now from the previous one, and Pete carried Bentley out of the water and laid her down on the sand. He checked her airway, rolled her over, turned her face sideways, and pressed on her back, but no water came out. He rolled her onto her back again and breathed into her, feeling silly, knowing from past experience with dead bodies that she was dead, but oh, how different this particular "dead" was! It seemed obscene to Pete as he looked down at the limp form, its youth screaming out at him, that the seventeen years Bentley Brown had lived were all the years she was ever going to get. He wasn't quite able to believe it. He found himself thinking suddenly of himself at seventeen, just starting out with the business of Factotum, doing many of the same odd jobs Bentley had been doing for him, looking back at what the years between seventeen and thirty-six had continued to offer him and would never, now, be offering her.

It took the police a long time to come. The island of Nashtoba had only three policemen, and except for the fire chief, the firemen who manned the rescue truck were all volunteer; still, it was a small island, and it seemed to take them a long time to come. He finally saw them approaching the beach from across the marsh in order of rank—first the huge, looming shape of the police chief, Willy McOwat, with the more wispy Paul Roose behind him, then the new young policeman, Ted Ball, who was the son of the oldest volunteer fireman. Yes, Ted's father, Ernie, was there, trailing behind the police with a stretcher, and the fire chief trotted along beside it carrying a box. Halfway onto the beach young Ted overtook the sixty-four-year-old Paul Roose, but he didn't seem able or willing to pass the chief, and Pete spent a few seconds trying to decide how a big man like the chief could be so light on his feet. As soon as he was within range, Pete asked after Maxine, and Willy McOwat jerked his thumb back over the marsh toward Pete's house and Factotum. The others had caught up to them by now and were elbowing Pete out of the way; Pete was more than happy to leave them to it.

"I'll be home," he said to Willy, and then shuffled, suddenly exhausted, back up the beach, watching his wet sneakers coat themselves with sand, feeling the eely wet denim of his jeans plastered against his legs. He took the shortest route straight through the tide pools and onto the marsh, along the cordgrass that edged the creek, then across the field of salt hay and up onto his lawn to find Maxine.

After she had made her call to the police, Maxine continued to sit at her mother's desk, not moving. Her mother's desk. Factotum. It was a strange little company that Pete and her mother ran, and Maxine had always thought it would be fun to work there until her mother decided she liked the idea too; immediately all the fun seemed to drain right out of it, and it became what it must have been to Maxine's mother all along—a way for her to keep an eye on her daughter on weekends and after school. The phone on the desk rang just then, and without thinking, Maxine picked it up. "Hello," she said, and then she added, remembering where she was, "Factotum." And in case it sounded as unofficial as it felt, she continued, quoting Pete's ad, "Persons employed to do all kinds of work."

"Who's this?" asked a deep male voice that sounded even older than her mother's.

"Maxine Peck."

"Maxine! Let me talk to your mother, honey. It's Bert Barker."

"She's not here," said Maxine, and she hung up the phone. She couldn't stand Bert.

Where *was* her mother? Maxine looked around at her mother's desk, trying to keep her mind off the scene at the beach. There was a neat stack of message pads, and the pile of papers all squared off even at the corners, and the tin full of pencils and pens, all neatly sharpened or capped, of course, and there was the picture of herself when she was fourteen that she hated.

The phone rang again, but Maxine didn't answer it. What would Pete have her do if she did work here? she wondered. They really did do all kinds of work: cleaning, painting, repairing things, driving people places, and even reading to that old Abrew lady Pete liked so much—but Maxine wasn't a very neat painter and she hated to clean and she couldn't drive yet and Pete would never let her take over the reading job . . .

Maxine was crying again, and hard. The tears were pouring down her face and she was actually shaking, and she didn't want her mother to see her this way. She got up. She would go back down to the beach and find Pete. And Bentley? No! All of a sudden the thought of seeing her mother didn't sound half so bad to Maxine, but she walked down the hall, out of the office part into Pete's private part, the part where he lived, and sat down at his kitchen table. Attached to the kitchen was a long porch, and the porch faced the marsh and the water and the . . . There they were, the police, running across the marsh toward the beach, carrying things. Maxine turned away, and just then the door to the office burst open and she could hear her mother's breathless gasp, "Maxine!"

Maxine stopped crying and wiped her face. She walked carefully and calmly out into the office again.

"Maxine!" Her mother's eyes were huge, hollow black pits of worry. *Lord,* how her mother could worry! "The ambulance! You're all right? Is it Pete?"

"It's Bentley," said Maxine, proud of the matter-of-factness in her own voice as compared to the panic in her mother's. "She drowned on the beach and Pete's with her, but I was the one who found her."

Maxine's mother closed her eyes and put a hand on her chest. She always did that, always came up with some gag right out of an old movie; the only trouble was, it was never a gag with her mother, it was just the way she was. It drove Maxine crazy.

"Bentley! Bentley Brown! And Pete's with her?" Her mother half turned toward the door.

"You shouldn't go down there. The cops are . . ." What *are* the cops doing? Was it possible they were reviving her? Somehow Maxine, who had never before seen death, was sure that this time she had seen it.

"Oh," said her mother, and all of a sudden her feet kind of shot straight out from under her and she sank backward onto the couch as if it were sheer coincidence that the couch was there to catch her at all. "That poor man," said Rita. "Another one! And he's not yet back to normal from the first one yet!"

Her own mother still wasn't completely back to normal from that first one, thought Maxine, but that's assuming that anyone by any stretch of the imagination could ever call her mother normal in the first place.

Pete started when the doctor, Hardiman Rogers, pulled his Volvo up out front, and he watched from the window as his gaunt frame, topped by a Mark Twain head of hair with eyebrows and mustache to match, lumbered off toward the beach after the others. His car was the last to arrive, but shortly after, the first to leave, and Pete, sensing that soon Bentley's body would follow, managed to herd Rita and Maxine out into the kitchen just in time for them to miss the loading and departing of the ambulance. He made Maxine a cup of tea and gave Rita a glass of wine but took nothing for himself; they waited, hovering around the old pine kitchen table, keeping their backs to the window that faced the now empty marsh, silent and uncomfortable. They knew the police chief would be walking down the hall any minute.

But he didn't. Instead they heard a knock on Factotum's outside door, proof once again that the chief was from Someplace Else. No one ever knocked on Factotum's door, they just opened it and walked in, and if it was after hours, and it was Pete they wanted, they knocked on the door at the end of the hall that led into his kitchen. Pete hurried out into the office, which had at one point been his living room and was still full of lumpy rattan furniture and old floor lamps, and opened the door for the chief.

The chief opened his mouth, but instead of speaking, he laid a heavy hand on Pete's shoulder, and Pete understood what that gesture meant—for just a minute this was the friend, not the police chief—then he shook his head, as if in disbelief, and the chief was back in charge.

"A few questions, if you don't mind," said Willy. "And is Maxine still here? I should have a statement from her also."

"In the kitchen," said Pete, and he led the way down the hall, not in the least anxious to talk further about the body on the beach, but the minute he entered the kitchen and saw Maxine's white face under its disarranged short black hair, he found himself starting right in, hoping that he could get all the talking out of the way for both of them.

"She was about twenty-five feet out from where I put her on the sand," he began, and the chief pulled up a chair at the table, took out a note pad, and began to write. "She was caught up in the rocks. She—"

"I thought she was a balloon," said Maxine. "I thought Bentley's sweater was a balloon."

"Did you see anyone on the marsh?" Willy asked them, and Pete and Maxine looked at each other, and both shook their heads.

"No one?"

Maxine gave Pete a look that seemed to say, "He thinks if he asks it twice, we'll say something he likes better the second time?" but out loud she said only, "No one." She

7

seemed to have all at once become composed beyond belief.

"Do you know why she was out there on the marsh?"

Maxine shook her head, but Pete spoke up. "Bentley and Carlisle have been working here weekends and after school all fall. They usually come by bus after school, but on weekends they sometimes borrow their mother's car or walk down the beach. I didn't see a car today, so I assume that's what she was doing, walking home from here. She left around three, wasn't it, Rita?"

Rita nodded, her eyes welling with tears as she spoke. Maxine, Pete noticed, looked away from her.

"And why was it that the two of you were on the marsh?"

Rita answered that one for them. "Maxine was a little out of sorts, weren't you, dear? And Pete suggested they go down to the beach together for some air, didn't you, Pete?"

Maxine faced her mother and glared, her mouth open and ready to speak, and Pete hurried to intercept her. "I felt like a walk," he said.

"Later Carlisle and Travis were going to drive me to the Shack," said Maxine, and now Rita glared and Maxine had perked up. The Shack, the diner where some of the high school students had taken to hanging out, was not one of Rita's favorite places.

"Carlisle and Travis?" asked the chief.

"Travis Dearborn," said Rita. "Travis and Carlisle are dating right now." And Maxine snorted at, Pete assumed, her mother's somewhat antique phraseology.

"And I suppose you're both sure this was Bentley?"

"As a matter of fact," said Pete, "I was never any good at telling them apart, but Maxine seemed to think—"

"It was Bentley," said Maxine, staring at Pete with surprise.

"They *are* identical?" said the chief. "She was in the water. I would assume there would be some confusion, at first, as to the—"

"It was Bentley," said Maxine.

"How do you know?"

Maxine looked around the table at all of them in apparent disbelief. She shrugged her shoulders.

"Bentley had her colors done," she said finally, and something of the reality of it must have struck home to her just then—the tears splashed down her cheeks in an instant flood, she pushed her chair back from the table, banging it into the wall, and stumbled out of the room. Rita jumped up to follow.

"I'm taking that child home," she said, with a look of grim determination that Pete never argued with, and the chief didn't argue with it either.

After they had gone, Pete and the chief remained at the table without speaking for some minutes.

"She was a strong swimmer," said Pete finally.

"Swimming wasn't going to help her much," said Willy, and something about the way he said it and about the way he wiped his face with a thick hand gave Pete a queasy feeling in the pit of his stomach, but still, he persevered a moment longer.

"I know she was in her clothes, but kids do that, I've done it. You're walking along, you see that water, you want a quick swim, it doesn't make any difference if your clothes get wet for once, that's half the fun of it. You—"

"Multiple blows to the head," said Willy, and now Pete wiped his own face with his own hands.

"She was caught in the rocks; maybe she hit her head on one when she dove in . . ."

*"Multiple,"* said Willy. "Repeated blows to the same area at the back of her head. You think she dove, stood up, dove, stood up, hitting the same spot each time? On the *back* of her head? And besides, Hardy says she was dead before she hit the water."

"No," said Pete, meaning no, this wasn't happening, couldn't be happening here. Not here, not on his quiet little island that had been so safely removed from the world by the flooding tides that had washed away the spit of land

9

that joined Nashtoba to the rest of Cape Hook. It was that damned wooden causeway, thought Pete; if they burned that bridge, then these things wouldn't come here, these off-islanders, these deaths . . . "Poor Bentley," he said finally, and the chief seemed to snap to attention, returning to the lost thread.

"Yeah, Bentley. Now, what's this 'she had her colors done' bit?"

Pete shrugged. He had no idea.

"Maxine hangs out with that crowd? Aren't they older, those twins and the Dearborn kid?"

Pete looked at Willy and sighed. There seemed to be no end of things that needed to be explained to the chief, but exactly how to do it? If Pete told him that this island of Nashtoba wasn't like Someplace Else, would that do it? If he explained that around here you didn't have blocks of kids to choose from, suburbs full of kids your own age so that you could ignore the younger ones the way you were supposed to when you were seventeen, would that suffice? "It isn't like that here," Pete said finally. "You don't worry so much about age around here. You hang around with the kids you want to hang around with. Carlisle and . . . Carlisle works here, and Maxine hangs around here a fair amount, it's not so—"

"Maxine was friendly with them both?"

Pete considered. Now that he thought about it, it had been mostly Carlisle and her boyfriend Travis who had ferried Maxine around, and he told the chief so.

"And how about access to this beach by car? How close to this place can you park a car?"

Pete shook his head. "It's a pretty deserted stretch; the marsh backs up to it all along, and it's pretty boggy out there. Four-wheel drive, maybe, but you'd have to know just where you were, watch the tide . . ."

Still, the chief seemed to have something in mind that involved cars. "How about the twins? You say they borrowed their mother's car on occasion. I take it they had no car of their own?"

Pete shook his head. "There aren't too many high school kids with their own cars around here; not a lot of jobs, not a lot of bucks floating around."

The chief stood up. "If, while Maxine is 'hanging around,' she says anything to enlighten us about the colors business, I'd appreciate it if you'd pass it along."

Pete stood up also, and walked behind Willy into the hall. He couldn't think of a reason why the chief would want to know about the colors so much. "The colors? You want to know about the colors?"

"The colors. And if you find out anything else, I'd appreciate that being passed along also."

So nothing had changed.

The little island of Nashtoba had not welcomed this new police chief from Boston with open arms. The island was like a family, the chief like the nosy neighbor in their eyes; family secrets were passed on freely within the family, but never outside. Nobody had ever volunteered anything to the chief, and it appeared he was still convinced that nobody ever would. Pete, an island native, hadn't had that problem; he got told more things than he ever wanted to know, and he was linked to almost every facet of island life by hundreds of years of self-imposed isolation, a live and kicking rumor mill, and his business of Factotum. What they didn't come right out and tell him, he absorbed directly through his skin, and it hadn't taken Willy McOwat long to figure all that out. Pete sighed. Sometimes he wished he had picked, or had been picked by, someone else as a friend. Sometimes he wished he lived somewhere else. He also wished, very much, that people didn't die, or leave, or change.

After the chief left to give the bad news to Bentley's mother, Pete took off his soaking clothes and threw them in the washing machine. At least that wasn't something that had changed, at least he wasn't one of those divorced men who, after his wife left him, couldn't boil water or iron his own shirts, who had to add that adjustment to the rest of the pain. But Pete wasn't up to thinking about Connie right now. After he set the wash in motion, he spent a good half hour wasting water in the shower, but all it washed away was some salt and a lot of sand.

Pete sat alone on Ree Brown's couch, wondering, again, what exactly he had hoped to be able to offer this woman by coming here. Carlisle Brown sat in one chair across from Pete, and Ree sat in the other. Travis Dearborn stood behind Carlisle and looked at the door with longing. Nobody was doing any talking.

"Listen," said Pete finally. "Aren't there any other relatives who could stay with you?"

"No," said Carlisle and Ree all at once, and Pete looked back and forth between them. Carlisle's short red hair, which was usually bouncy with curls, now seemed to hang limp, her white skin was almost blue around her eyes, and the blue eyes themselves were pink-rimmed. She was wearing her usual attire—ripped jeans, a long sweater that stopped inches above the rolled-up cuffs of her jeans, and a short vest with buttons sewn all over it. *Bentley had her colors done*. What *did* that mean? He conjured up the last image of the pink and cream Bentley, whose socks matched her sweater and whose sneaks matched her socks. Pete looked at Carlisle again, at her face, and nothing in it moved.

Ree's face, on the other hand, was another matter, lumpy and almost jumping with pain. The twins' hair had obviously come from her, but hers was a deeper red that was streaked with silver. She had attempted to pin up the wild curls, but the pins were already backing out, and corkscrews of hair dripped down around her neck. She had hazel eyes that seemed to vary in color as he watched, and their expression filled her whole face with grief.

"Listen, Ree," said Pete again. He couldn't look at her without wracking his brain for ways to help, but what could he do? What could he offer? He didn't know this woman's innermost nature, he didn't know how she would be taking all this, he only knew how he would be taking it, how he was taking it, and he was connected by only a brief and fairly superficial relationship with the girl. "Would you like to get out of here for a while?"

Ree suddenly sprang up out of her chair. "No. Please. I . . ." She looked with desperation at her daughter, and then all at once her strength seemed to leave her. Pete jumped up and steadied her as she sagged back into her chair. "I just can't lose another one," she said, and Pete was at once reminded of this woman's other loss, her fisherman husband who had been lost at sea eight years before, and he didn't know what to say or do. Something now seemed to snap Carlisle back to life, however, and she stood up and took hold of her mother's arm.

"Come on, Mom, why don't you go lie down? Trav? Help me?"

Travis scrambled over to the other side, awkwardness masking what Pete knew to be a near-professional athleticism. Between them they helped Ree up and began to lead her from the room while Pete stood up and hovered like a spare Goodyear blimp.

Travis was the first one to return to the room, and Pete noticed for the first time how really awful Travis looked. His tall, handsome body seemed to droop, his dark hair looked dull, his skin was shiny with sweat, and he continued to look at the door as if it were his only friend. He appeared lost, as if he did not have the faintest clue what was expected of him; he wanted out, and at that moment Pete almost felt sorrier for Travis than he did for the sister he was there to help. When Carlisle came back into the room, Pete intercepted a quick flash of impatience in her face, and he began to suspect she would just as soon be rid of Travis.

Pete tried. "Is there anything we can do, Carlisle? Make some phone calls, do some errands, give anybody a ride?" He looked at Travis, and as he had hoped, Travis was able to pick up on a good idea when he heard one.

"Yeah! I can do some errands," he said. Carlisle looked

at the two of them and seemed to make a decision as to who was most in need of getting out.

"Thanks, Trav," she said. "Dr. Rogers has something at the drugstore for Mom. You want to go get it?"

Travis was gone before she'd quite finished the sentence, and the minute he left, Carlisle sank down onto the couch behind Pete and began that choking, coughing noise that people make when they're not quite comfortable about having a cry.

There was a knock at the door. At first it didn't look like Carlisle wanted to answer it, but when a voice on the other side said, "Carlisle?" she jumped up.

Pete had seen this fellow before, but knew only his name and nothing more about him. Henry Tourville was very tall, taller than Travis, thin and awkward-looking and blinking behind large glasses, but he seemed to possess an instinct for the situation that Travis had lacked. The arms that he put around Carlisle were not hesitant in the least, and she seemed to know that once she was safe inside them, it was okay to cry there.

And Pete knew it was okay to leave.

So he did.

# Chapter
# 2

Connie Bartholomew stepped out of the bashed-up Triumph, pulled the crotch of her jeans down and the sleeves of her thick wool sweater up, and shook her hair out over her shoulders. She looked up. The lineup on Beston's porch was the same as ever—the obese and shiny-pale Ed Healey on the left, then that snaky Bert Barker, then Evan Spender's weathered and craggy features, the heads of all three looking in her direction while the mouths went sideways toward each other. They seemed to be appreciating her, but still, she was kind of sorry she had been pulling at her crotch like that—she could see the whole thing mushroom out off Beston's porch and over the island in the next cloud of gossip that happened to sail by. Oh, hell, she thought, if you were being bisected up the middle, you were entitled to unbisect yourself, and there was enough going on around here so that her crotch would really have to fall pretty far down on the list. Of course, she wouldn't have had to be pulling at herself at all if she could just stop *eating* all the time . . . Either the thought of her somewhat recently acquired food habits or the greeting that sailed her way from Beston's porch suddenly reminded her of her ex-husband, and caused her to break her stride.

"Well, Mrs. Bartholomew," called Bert Barker. He

called her that just to bug her, knowing how she hated those attachments to the fronts of names, knowing how awkward it was now that she was legally no longer Pete's wife.

"Oh, shut up, Bert," said Connie, but she winked at Evan and nodded to Ed. She went into Beston's and purchased a hammer and a box of nails, returned to the porch, got a Coke from the rusty machine that still sold them for a quarter, leaned against the rail next to Evan, and settled down to chat with the island's un-, under-, and never-employed.

"You did a real nice job on the lawn," said Ed. "Nice to have you back working for Factotum. Kept wanting to tell Pete what a nice job you did till I remember what you made me promise. Can't say's I see the sense in it, but there it is, a promise."

"That's right," said Connie. "You keep your big yap shut, all right?"

"No," said Ed, "it isn't all right. But there it is, a promise."

"Heard about Bentley?" asked Bert, and Connie almost snorted out a laugh until she realized that it was not a laugh-producing subject. How could she not have heard about Bentley around this place?

"Well, I hope somebody tells Willy," said Bert, and the other men chuckled, but Connie frowned. She had been back on the island only a few months after all, but she was getting a little bit sick of these jokes at the new chief's expense. Was it because she was an outsider herself, accepted initially only because of the island's high regard for Pete, reaccepted now because . . . Why? Because she had come back? Because they all assumed she had come back *to him?* And that was another question, why she had come back.

"Autopsy report came in yesterday aft," said Ed. "Multiple blows to the head, just like Hardy told 'em. And pregnant."

Now, that was news to Connie, but some perverse part

of her nature didn't want to let Ed know it. She stared down into her Coke, admiring the long, tall glass bottle that you didn't find around much anymore. Yes, there were some things that were good about being back . . .

"Still teacher-certified?" Evan Spender asked from his corner. Evan wasn't much like the other porch roosters, the alcoholic Ed Healey or the mooch-off-his-wife Bert Barker; Evan actually worked as a telephone repairman, although no one ever saw him doing it much. Evan could keep his mouth shut sometimes, and when he didn't keep his mouth shut, like as not you were just as glad that he hadn't, so when he asked Connie this question, she knew enough to answer it.

"Yes, although a lot of good it does me. Why?"

Evan shrugged his shoulders and sipped his Coke and squinted at the sky, and just when Connie had decided it wasn't worth waiting for any longer, he cleared his throat. "That new young high school teacher's pregnant."

Connie thrust her Coke bottle into the carton in disgust. "For chrissake, Evan, I can't hang around here unemployed for nine more months on the off chance she decides maternity leave isn't going to be long enough!"

Evan seemed to give that a good long minute's thought, and for once, neither of the other two men interrupted him. "No," Evan agreed.

That was it.

Connie glared at him.

"Went to Hardy's last week and got told something's wrong with her cervix."

Ed Healey looked down at the ground, shuffled his feet, and coughed once or twice. You didn't talk about things like cervixes in front of Ed.

Connie took three deep breaths. She could tell Evan still had more coming, but waiting him out was not one of her particular talents. "Well, I'm sorry to hear that, Evan," she said, "but I'm not about to run on over there with flowers, now, am I?"

Evan seemed to consider that remark for some time, then

shook his head, looked out over Main Street, and went on. "Hardy's sent her on home to bed."

Connie grabbed the porch post hard, and asked very sweetly, she thought, "So what, Evan?"

Evan looked her square in the eye. "For six months."

Connie looked back at him.

"Can't get up out of bed for six months, not once or she'll lose it, Hardy says, and Evelyn Smoot isn't much pleased with that Betty Birdsall, who's been subbing. She's looking around, I'm told."

Evelyn Smoot was the school principal. But who was this Betty Birdsall? "Who the hell is Betty Birdsall?"

"Newcomer," Ed Healey answered her. "Lives out by the causeway road. Married to Percy Platt."

Betty Platt, who had arrived on Nashtoba in 1947 and married Percy ten years later, was still called Betty Birdsall, the newcomer, while Connie herself would go to her grave as Mrs. Peter Bartholomew! Now, why *was* that?

"Birdsall ran study halls all day yesterday, and Evie didn't much care for that. You might just fit the bill. If I were you, I'd hop right on over there this morning."

*You might just fit the bill.* Connie looked down at the hammer and nails in her hand and sighed. What did that mean, this hammer and nails? It meant that she was going home to her two rooms over the Coolidges' garage to hang up a few pictures. And what did hanging up a few pictures mean? It meant she was thinking about settling in. And what did *that* mean? It meant she was going to need a job and she was going to need one fast. Pete was out of the hospital and back at work now, so she wasn't going to be helping out at Factotum anymore. He wouldn't want her there, for one thing, and she didn't want to work there, for another; not that the summer hadn't been kind of fun, working again with Rita and the twins . . .

All of a sudden Connie felt that quick crush of gloom that the news of Bentley's death had first given her, and thought, almost at once, not of Bentley's mother or sister, who had lost her, but of Pete, who had found her. Poor Pete.

"Better watch it, Mrs. B," said Bert, and Connie jumped as if he'd been reading her thoughts. "First thing Smoot'll ask is where you were Saturday between the hours of three and five, and you better have an alibi. They're not gonna go hiring any kid killers, y'know, not to teach in the school."

Connie ignored Bert and continued to stare at Evan.

"You'd be all right," said Evan. "I'll be seeing Evelyn Smoot in an hour or two; I can put in a word if you're interested."

"Course," Bert Barker went on, "you can't pin old Hardy down to anything like *exactly* the time, now can you? Body was in the water, see, and you know how he loves to confuse things when you run into a little water. Water's too cold, water's too hot, could've been dead an hour, could've been dead two . . ."

Nobody was really listening to Bert. "Thanks, Evan," said Connie, and Evan nodded at her, his blue eyes still keen.

"After three, before five, he said, didn't he, Ed?" Bert continued on, but Connie bounced down the steps and off toward her car. "Hey, Mrs. B!" he hollered after her. "You look as good going as you do coming, y'know that?"

Connie hopped into her car and jammed her hair up into an old painter's hat that she had pilfered from Factotum.

"Y'know," Ed Healey boomed out from behind her, "I hate like hell to agree with you, Bert, but I'd guess in this case I've got to agree!"

Connie started the engine just then and consequently couldn't quite hear the one word from Evan on the matter, but it had had an affirmative sort of a sound to it, and she found herself feeling pretty perky as she drove away. After all, she thought, it had been a very successful stop; a job tip on one hand, and three middle-aged men deciding that she still looked pretty good. Connie hadn't felt particularly attractive in quite some time, and this last thought was strangely comforting. And of course, she told herself, let's not forget the whole reason for the stop in the first place! She now had her very own hammer and nails, and for some reason, the hammer and nails on the seat beside her seemed to take on the very essence of comfort itself.

Evelyn Smoot seemed eager enough to act on Evan Spender's recommendation; that very morning Connie found herself in the principal's office, but where she might have been on Saturday between the hours of three and five would have been easier to talk about than what they actually did discuss.

"Your previous teaching experience is—"

"Brief," interrupted Connie. She laughed. "I must say the kids loved me, but I haven't been able to elect any kids to a school committee yet."

"And for many years you did this Factotum . . ."

Connie looked out the office window at the scrub pines, and took a deep breath. "Well, it seemed like a good idea at the time. Then I married the guy, and then the marriage went bust, and it didn't seem like a good idea to stay on there after that, but I think if you asked him, he'd give me a good reference. About the work I did for Factotum, that is, not on being a wife." Connie grinned, but never in her life had a smile felt so uncomfortable.

"I know Peter Bartholomew. I remember him as a student also." Evelyn Smoot looked at Connie more closely. "I believe he would give you a good reference, at that."

Connie looked more closely at Evelyn Smoot. She was middle-aged, sturdy, gray, substantial, and expressionless. Connie was not at all sure if Smoot's remark was meant to be a compliment on her skills on the job, or a comment on Pete as a sucker.

Evelyn Smoot began to tap a paper on her desk with a sturdy finger, and Connie had a sinking feeling that the paper was her resume. "You say here that you are presently unemployed? I understood that you were once again working for Factotum. I understood that you have been—"

Connie interrupted again, vaguely aware that interruptions were not the most clever thing she could be doing, but she was unable to hear the word "Factotum" one more time. "No, I'm not."

Evelyn Smoot raised her eyebrows and looked at Connie with what seemed like very little enthusiasm.

Okay, thought Connie, you don't have to rub it in, just tell me to get out. She began to get up, but Mrs. Smoot looked so surprised that she sat back down at once.

"How badly do you want this job?" Evelyn Smoot asked, and the question surprised Connie almost as much as the answer that she heard herself giving back.

"Very much." God, it was true! Suddenly she did want this job very much. But why? So that she could hang around the island watching Pete duck her at every turn?

Evelyn Smoot looked at her for some seconds and then cleared her throat in a that-takes-care-of-that kind of way. "You will be teaching U.S. history, ancient history, and current events to the high school grades. I will expect your classes to be conducted with sufficient efficiency to have completed the curriculums despite getting off to a late, and possibly . . . unorthodox . . . start. How soon do you expect to be available? Assuming, of course, that the rest of your credentials check out?"

Connie stared at Evelyn Smoot. Then she looked at her watch. "If I skipped lunch, I guess I could make the one o'clock class."

Evelyn Smoot cleared her throat again, and this time it was not a that-takes-care-of-that kind of thing, it was more of an okay-here-it-comes kind of clearing.

"There is only one more thing I feel it necessary to discuss at this point. There has been, as I am sure you are aware, a death."

Connie swallowed. "Yes."

"You will have Carlisle Brown in your junior U.S. history class, but all the students in the school knew her sister as well, and I am sure we can expect some difficulties to arise as they struggle to grasp this situation. If you see any specific problems, I would like you to bring them at once to my particular attention. No one else's but mine. Is this perfectly clear to you? You will speak to me and me only?''

It seemed perfectly clear. It also reminded Connie once again that it was not easy to hide from tragedy on an island the size of this one.

"Do you have any questions?"

Yes, thought Connie. Does life make sense to you? But out loud she answered, "No."

To both questions.

# Chapter
## 3

Pete tried to get out of his bed with some semblance of bounce, but found that his extended stay in the hospital had pretty well unbounced him, or perhaps it was the death of Bentley Brown, or maybe it was yet another September morning lying ahead of him at Factotum. It was this last thought that finally pried him loose from the sheets. He *liked* Factotum. He liked this little cottage that held him and his business and his life so compactly and, well, maybe not so neatly, but there it was. Just because it had once held more than himself and his business didn't mean that it wasn't as attractive as it had ever been. Just because Connie had left him for Glen Newcomb, another Factotum employee, shouldn't make this little Cape cottage with all its bookshelves and pine floors and cypress walls any less exactly what he had always wanted in a house. True, Connie had occasionally expressed interest in something more, something other, something less *congested*.

But enough was enough. He was over that now. He was over *her*, and so, apparently, was Glen Newcomb, but that was nothing to do with Pete anymore, Connie was nothing to do with him anymore. For a minute a picture of her in the old rocking chair on the porch drinking a Ballantine with her feet propped up on the rail slowed his footsteps and had him looking with hope at the door; then he shook his head and strode into the bathroom and stared at his face in the mirror.

He still looked hospital-pale; his once well-muscled torso was thin and consequently made his six-foot frame seem longer. The scar that ran from the bottom of his rib cage around his side and almost into his armpit still looked raw, and if he were going to tell the truth instead of the usual lie that he told anyone who asked, he still hurt when he moved the wrong way. Scar tissue, Hardy Rogers had said. Scar tissue between the ribs that would get inflamed and press on the nerves and cause him to clutch at his chest and groan if no one was looking or to break out in a cold sweat and remain deadly still if anyone was. Pete turned away from the mirror, having exceeded his limit for looking at his own reflection some seconds ago. He decided to shower before he shaved this morning, feeling the need of a bit of a break before he faced the mirror, and by the time he was standing in front of it again, he was already feeling a little more squarely set.

First things first. He shaved the shadow off his face and felt at once less pale. He flicked his dark brown hair with its tinge of red straight back with a comb, but didn't spend much time doing it, knowing that before he left the bathroom, it would be doing whatever it wanted to anyway. He put on an old navy blue corduroy bathrobe that was ripped at one shoulder and along both seams, left the bathroom, and walked through the kitchen and out onto the porch to check out the morning air. It was, as he expected, Nashtoba-in-September cold; at eight o'clock in the morning he could still just see his breath, and his bare feet on the worn floorboards were requesting an immediate about-face into the kitchen. He gave the marsh and the gray-green ribbons of water beyond it only a fleeting glance this morning and, returning inside, made himself a cup of instant coffee, downed a glass of juice, constructed a mountainous bowl of Wheaties and bananas, and carried it with him back to the bedroom to eat as he dressed. He rooted through his drawers looking for the thick flannel shirt that his scouting mission to the porch had told him the day required, and frowned when he couldn't find it until he remembered he had worn it that day on the beach with Maxine. He had washed the salt and sand off all those clothes soon after, and had not seen them since; the shirt was most likely still balled up in the dryer. He put down his Wheaties and ripped the sheets off the bed, figuring if he was going to go near the washing machine, he might as well use it. He threw open the top of the machine, leaned over to make sure it was empty, and there in the bottom he saw it, that flash of gold sparkling from the depths of his washing machine in much the same way it had flashed up at him at the beach. He reached in, scooped it up, and looked at it. Around the faceted blue stone, raised gold letters spelled out "Nashtoba High School." Despite the fact that the school went from kindergarten on up, the rings given out to the seniors always said "Nashtoba High School," and the students in the higher grades were always called high school students. On each side of the band of letters was a carved hawk, the school's symbol. The Nashtoba Hawks. Pete had once been one, and below the hawks on Pete's ring was a date that was now close to being twenty years old. The date on the ring in his hand was still in the future, a year ahead. As Pete stared down at the carved gold, suddenly everything he had pushed into the back of his mind reclaimed its proper place. He would have to see Willy about this. Soon.

Pete finished dressing and went into the bathroom to brush his teeth, this time not looking into the mirror at all. Then he went through the kitchen, down the hall, and into the front room, which had once been his living room. He walked up to the desk where Rita was already working and sat down on the corner of it.

Pete had hired Rita Peck many years before for what at the time had seemed the simple job of answering Factotum's phone. Now ten years and one divorce apiece later, Rita was a full partner, and from that same spot in the corner where she insisted on remaining, she pulled and prodded and pummeled the business of Factotum, and sometimes Pete himself, into shape.

"Morning, Rita," he said. "How's Maxine?" Rita looked up at him from under a smooth wing of jet black hair and frowned the frown that usually meant something like Maxine-went-to-school-in-twenty-degree-weather-without-wearing-any-socks.

"She's fine," said Rita. "She's absolutely fine." But the frown took a turn into the I-just-found-a-vodka-bottle-in-her-underwear-drawer range.

"What's the matter?"

"What's the *matter!* Doesn't that seem like something's the matter to you? Wouldn't you think that a fifteen-year-old girl who had just found the dead body of her friend on the beach would be something other than *fine?* I'm trying to tell you, Pete, she's *fine!*"

"Oh," said Pete.

"I mean of course she isn't *fine,* we both know perfectly well she isn't *fine,* but she's *acting* like she is. You know what I mean." Rita ran long, scarlet fingernails through her hair and left it, if anything, neater than it had been before. "I just don't know what to do about her, Pete. She won't talk to me. Not about this, not about anything. I said to her, don't you want to talk about it? and she started *shrieking* at me! I knew this was going to happen, she said. I knew the minute I saw Bentley that you were going to do this. You were going to try to *talk* to me about it! I mean for crying out loud! What does she *think* I would try to do, *ignore* it?"

"Maybe that's what she needs to do right now, ignore it. Maybe she's just not ready to talk."

"She'll *never* be ready to talk to me. And her father's no use. Leave her alone, he said, when I called to tell him. Leave her alone and let her work it out herself! I *ask* you! A fifteen-year-old girl, working it out herself!"

"Is she coming by this afternoon? Maybe I could—"

Suddenly the frown flew away and Rita's brown eyes

smoothed down into calm pools. "She's supposed to take the bus straight home today, but I could call school and leave a message for her to get off here." Determined fingers were already reaching for the phone.

"Good," said Pete. "Now I've got to go talk to Willy. I forgot all about it, but I found this on the beach on Saturday right near where Maxine found Bentley." He pulled the ring out of his pocket, and both he and Rita looked at it silently for a moment, then Rita pulled herself up straighter in her chair, smoothed down her sweater, and reached again for the phone.

"Right," she said, but as Pete slid off her desk and moved toward the door, he could hear her voice taking on a they-just-told-me-you-checked-yourself-out-of-the-hospital-a-day-early kind of tone.

"You are absolutely *scrawny,* do you know that? I *swear,* I think you got used to those IVs in the hospital and now you won't give decent food a try. Don't you ever *eat?*"

"I eat," said Pete, suddenly remembering with longing a now soggy bowl of Wheaties resting on top of his dresser, and leaving him with nothing to say.

But once he saw the ring in Pete's hand and had listened to his story, the police chief had plenty to say. "You mean to tell me I've been tracking teenagers all over this island when I should have been doing your laundry?"

"I'm sorry," said Pete.

"And you washed it. You washed it in the washing machine, is that what you're trying to say?"

"I'm sorry," said Pete again.

The chief ran a large hand over a long jaw and grumbled on. "Can you at least show me where you found the thing?"

"Of course," said Pete, trying to sound insulted enough to regain some of his self-respect.

Willy stood up, immediately dwarfing his desk, and strode toward the office door. As he passed the desk of the dispatcher, Jean Martell, he said, "I'll be at the beach. Half hour." It didn't seem necessary to indicate what beach, and it also didn't seem likely that Jean would suspect him of trying to catch a quick swim, but she did have a few questions. Jean Martell always had a few questions. Pete looked at Willy as he talked to Jean. Willy had a way of squinting when he was looking at you, as if he wanted to shut down the windows to his own thoughts as much as he could while at the same time narrowing the beam until it could pierce straight through your own skull and into your brain. Pete had taken it as a sign of an escalating friendship that it had been some time since he had had The Squint beamed on him.

Finally the chief moved on, but before Pete could escape in his wake, Jean caught at his sleeve, giving him a cozy smile that didn't go with the severe bun cemented to the top of her head. She waved a hand at a row of shelves behind her. "She did a good job, didn't she?"

"Who?"

"Connie, of course. But don't tell her I told you! Though why the big secret, I'm sure I can't see, I mean after all . . ."

Connie? The chief's head and shoulders reappeared around the door up ahead and looked interrogatively at Pete. Pete gratefully followed him out into the open air.

Connie?

It was the fault of the tide, more than anything. It was a different time on a different day; the tide pools that had been there were there no longer, and the few rocks that had tipped the waves were now projecting at crazy angles all over the place. Pete and Willy tramped around in the September chill, and after a lot of ineffectual pacing, Pete ventured a guess. "Here," he said with confidence, and the ruts across the chief's forehead smoothed out. "I think," he added, and the chief's forehead rerutted. The chief was a man of few words, and those few were usually

carefully picked and well modulated, but Pete was beginning to realize that everyone can change.

"We've combed this whole beach three times, and I
don't feel like doing it more than once again. Here, you
say. You *think*."

Pete, in the meantime, had made some tidal projections
and was feeling more sure, as sure as he'd felt about anything of late, which wasn't saying a whole lot. "This is the
place here," he said more forcefully. "I *think*."

The chief looked around, bent down, stood up, looked
around some more, turned around and faced Factotum, and
started to walk. Twenty feet away he turned around and
looked at Pete, and Pete, now getting the idea that they
were leaving, hustled after him up the rise of the beach.
Just as they hit the old straws of seaweed that had washed
up onto the marsh, Willy dug into the pocket of his khaki
pants and pulled out the ring, turning it over as he continued up the path. "Hardy says the body was moved.
Dragged. Afterward."

"Oh," said Pete.

Willy held the ring up to the pale sky and squinted at it.
"So someone's missing a ring."

"It's next year's class," said Pete. "Some junior's."
Bentley was a junior.

Willy tried it on his thick finger, letting it rest a third of
the way down on the ring finger of his left hand. "Some
guy, most likely?"

"Some guy," Pete reiterated. He, too, had tried the ring
and found it a fairly good fit. "They must have a list somewhere of who ordered rings. There aren't any initials. In
my day we put initials inside. In my day you didn't get
your ring until senior year, either." In his day? Pete was
feeling lately that his day was long over.

"Bentley's boyfriend," said Willy. "It could belong to
Bentley's boyfriend, and Bentley could have been wearing
it, right?"

Pete frowned. In his day that had been common enough,
too—the boyfriend gives the girlfriend his ring, the girl-

friend wears it on a chain around her neck or holds it on her finger with her own smaller class ring serving as a ring guard—but he tried to remember if he had ever seen or heard of Bentley with a boyfriend and could not recall it. "I don't think she had a boyfriend."

"She had one," said Willy. "At least she had one once. At least for fifteen minutes somewhere she did. She was pregnant."

Pete groaned.

"Of course, ask a bunch of kids and nobody has any idea who he could be. Nobody will admit she ever even talked to a boy; even her mother and her sister can't imagine who it could have been, had no idea she was pregnant . . ." Willy looked around, first at the expanse of marsh, then at the beach swept clean by the last moon tide, then at Pete, as if Pete had something more to tell him, some secret route by which a car might have come here and left no tracks. "I suppose one person could drag a seventeen-year-old-girl far enough. I don't suppose he'd need help. I don't suppose she got lugged too far, not unless a car got down here far enough to drop her off someplace . . ."

Pete shrugged.

They were three-quarters of the way over the marsh when Willy stopped and turned to face Pete.

"Your wife doesn't like me too much."

Pete coughed to cover his surprise and began to choke. When he recovered, he said, "Ex-wife." He'd been saying that a lot lately, it seemed.

They resumed walking. "Is she antagonistic toward the police in general, is that it?"

"I was not aware that she was particularly antagonistic . . ."

The chief gave a great laughing snort. "She's teaching at the school, but you know that, I guess."

This time Pete was the one who stopped. "No, I didn't."

"Well, she is." The chief moved them on, verbally as well as physically.

"Well, somebody knows who got Bentley pregnant, and that's the guy who did it. If he's missing his ring . . ."

They were almost up to the lawn of Factotum now, and again the chief stopped and turned to stare at Pete, his eyes cloudy gray troughs surrounded by crow's-feet. "And how are *you* getting along with your wife these days?"

"Ex-wife," said Pete, again. "Haven't seen her. And why do you ask?"

But all he got for an answer was The Squint.

The memory of the shelves in the police station was nagging at Pete. He had been meaning to do that job, it had been on the list that Rita doled out to him, so why had *Connie* done it? And why wasn't he supposed to know? He was driving past Mable's Coffee Shop when he happened to notice Mable's sign, something else that had been on the list for that summer, the repainting and rehanging of it, and there it was, bright and shining and swinging in the fall breeze. He cranked the wheel sharply, pulled in to Mable's, got out of the truck, and walked around the sign once. "Mable's," it said. "Hot Coffee. Fresh Donuts." In fresh paint.

"Nice job, huh?" said Mable from behind the counter, jangling questionably bright blond braids for a woman of sixty-three. "Two honey-dipped?"

Pete didn't bother to answer the donut question, since his usual order was already in the bag and a large coffee was steaming in front of him before he got through the door. "Who did it?"

Mable smacked what was left of her top teeth against what was left of her bottoms. "Connie did it. Smart job of it too, and in no time." The braids dangled free as she tipped her head to one side, the better to regard Pete. "Of course, for some reason that makes no sense far as I can see, I'm not supposed to tell you she did it, so button your lip, all right? Of course, when one person does something nice for another person . . . Hey!" Mable changed veins. "A shame about the Brown girl. Didn't know her much

31

myself, but she seemed a nice kid. Interested, you know? Listened to you. Now, who in the name of hell bashed her head in? There's some other kids I could name, you could see why someone might bash in *theirs* . . ."

Pete shoved his money across the counter before she could name them, but Mable shoved it back, barking across it at him, "Take your money and get out of here! If you think I'm charging you for two lousy day-old donuts and a cup of coffee I was about to toss down the sink . . ."

"Thank you, Mable," he said, and as she expected him to do, bit into one of the donuts and rolled his eyes in joy. "Day old, my foot," he said, also as expected, and he turned and left the coffee shop, carefully avoiding looking at the sign.

When he got back to Factotum, Pete expected to worm some explanations out of Rita, but for some reason, he couldn't seem to get much out of her. She had an urgent list of things for him to do—Henry Baker's cat had just had a seizure, and Pete had to get it and take it to the vet, then he had to read today's paper to Sarah Abrew, whose eyesight could no longer handle the fine print, and Rita had decided it would be just as well if Pete picked Maxine up at school instead of having her take the bus to Factotum. Pete listened to his list and noticed that once again, she had left off the things that usually fell to him to do—chop a cord of wood, clear an acre of brush, build a garage.

"I'm okay now, Rita, I keep telling you. Who's going to do Jerry's woods and the Peales' garage and the—"

"I'm working on that," said Rita, and then she conveniently picked up a ringing phone. She could drag out a phone call as long as necessary, Pete knew that, and at the moment it seemed that the best move was to get Henry's cat.

Maxine hunkered down into the seat of the old truck and meticulously pointed her face out the window on her side. Pete examined the bare nape of her neck, decided that it looked a little redder than usual, and concluded that she felt about as foolish over this whole thing as he did.

"Look," he began. "It was your mother's idea for me to pick you up, it wasn't her idea for me to want to talk to you."

"My mother is an idiot."

"Hey, wait a minute," said Pete. "This is a friend of mine you're talking about here, and I can vouch from personal experience that your mother is not even close to being an idiot. So when you're thinking again about mouthing off like that in my presence, please keep in mind you're talking about a buddy of mine and kindly—"

Maxine blew air at her window with a perfect snort of exasperation. "Right. Okay. So what do you want to tell me?"

"Tell you?" Pete must have succeeded in sounding surprised, since Maxine began to turn in his direction but then seemed to think better of it and checked her swing. "Ask you. Ask you, Max. I need some information. About class rings."

This time she couldn't resist. She turned her face to look at him, her downy eyebrows knitted into a softer version of her mother's, her eyes so hollow that it made Pete face his own window for a brief interlude himself. He sighed.

He had driven them from the school parking lot along Shore Road, the road that circled the island in a long and lazy loop, and had pulled up in the parking lot of Lupo's, asking Maxine if she wanted a soda. She had not. Pete, hungry as well as thirsty, sat in the truck and looked longingly through the windshield toward the restaurant's window booths.

*"What* rings?"

"Nashtoba High School rings. Who gets them, anyway? Isn't it supposed to be seniors? Your big reward for graduating? Your souvenir to take out into the world?"

Maxine snorted again, and for an instant her eyes opened into something more round and full of life. "Hah! What *senior* ever wore a ring out into the *world!* You don't wear a ring from your *high school* if you're off in college or something. That's why they give them to *juniors*. So you can get some use of it. Wear it around a couple years and then chuck it in an old box.''

"Or give it to your girlfriend?"

Now the eyes that she turned on Pete were first blank, then curious. "Give it to your *girlfriend?*"

"I mean only if you're a guy. If you're going steady. Give the girl your ring and she can wear it on a chain or—"

Maxine chortled. "Whose dumb idea is that?"

Pete coughed. Not that he had ever given a girl his ring or anything, not that it was his idea in the first place, but still he felt a little miffed. "So nobody does that anymore?"

"No way," said Maxine, and she adjusted her upper torso so that she could commune with her own window again.

Pete, who had been about to bring up the subject of Bentley now that Maxine had actually almost laughed a little, thought better of it, and continued on.

"Now, these rings. Don't you usually get your initials engraved inside? I thought everyone got their initials put inside them and—"

"Not this dumb, cheap, idiot school. They messed them up one year, and the company said it was the school's fault, and the school said it was the company's fault, and they wouldn't fix them without the school having to pay all over again, and after that, the school said no more monograms inside; if you wanted your ring monogrammed, you had to get it done yourself later. Nobody does, though." Now Maxine straightened herself up and swung right around in the seat and stared at Pete. "What are you asking all this stuff for, anyway?"

It seemed as good an opening as any. "The day we went walking and we found Bentley? I also found a class ring. First you hollered about the balloon, remember? I was standing on the edge of the water, I looked down and saw the ring and picked it up, and then you figured out it wasn't a balloon anymore and I ran after you and shoved the ring in my pocket and forgot all about it.''

Maxine was silent, but she was sitting straight in the seat now, staring ahead of her.

"It's a weird thing," continued Pete. "I've had nightmares about that scene, and never once did that part about me picking up the ring enter into it. I didn't remember it until I found it in the wash.''

Maxine's legs were crossed, and she began to snap the top foot into the side of the truck, right about where Pete figured the next rust hole would appear.

"I have nightmares, too," she said, still looking straight ahead. "Horrible nightmares. She keeps saying things to me, and not being dead, and I can't get her out of the water and she keeps *looking* at me! *Staring* at me!'' Maxine's eyes were shiny wet. "And then this other horrible thing happens. The chief comes and he keeps telling everyone I was the one who said Bentley was dead and then Bentley starts saying No! No! I'm not dead! Maxine, why are you doing this to me?'' Maxine turned to look at Pete. "Carlisle hasn't come to school," she said. "She hasn't come to work at Factotum either, has she?''

"Not yet," said Pete. "Give her time. Think how you feel. Then imagine what it's like for her.''

"Nobody thinks how awful it was, Pete, do they? Nobody thinks what it was like to find her.''

"I know," said Pete.

Neither of them spoke for some minutes, and then Pete decided to move on to other questions. "You said Bentley had her colors done. What does that mean?''

Maxine glanced at Pete with wonder, as if she still could not believe there was this other world in which people knew nothing at all about anything. "She had her colors done," she repeated. "Bentley's a spring. She's supposed to wear pink and yellow and turquoise and gold and things. She's a spring," she repeated, when Pete still looked confused.

"But Carlisle would be too, wouldn't she?" asked Pete

before he could stop himself, but the thought didn't seem to upset Maxine. She was actually sitting on one foot now, three-quarters of the way turned to Pete, and her skin, which had gone blue-white, was now very pink again.

"Of course she would, but Carlisle doesn't care, Carlisle just wears any old thing if she likes it, she doesn't care what color it is. Course, Bentley didn't so much either, not till she did this colors thing. And then she started wearing all this makeup. Didn't it look awful with her face all white like that and her . . ."

She stopped talking, and Pete saw the shine return to her eyes. It was time to change the tone.

"So what am I?" he asked. "Spring?"

Maxine looked up and down and gave him a fleeting flash of her small, orthodontically perfected teeth. "Spring! You think you're a spring? Autumn. You're one of those autumns. I think that green is supposed to be okay for you, that's a good kind of green, that shirt, for you." She studied him for another minute. "Really, I'd have to look it up, but you look okay to me."

She looked out her window again, her smile gone now, and she sighed a huge sigh. "I tell you," she said. "If I could stop having these stupid nightmares . . ."

Pete reached over and whacked her on the knee. "Don't worry about the nightmares, Max. You know how they wear you out? How you're so exhausted when you wake up from one?"

She nodded, watching him.

"Well, they do that to themselves after a while. They wear themselves out. You'll win in the end."

She turned back to the front of the truck, and remained, for one second, very still. "Bentley didn't," she said.

# Chapter
# 4

Connie leaned against the wall, crossed one sneakered foot over the other, and looked at her class. The island of Nashtoba traditionally housed all its students from all the grades in one old clapboard school building, adding onto the existing structure instead of breaking off and building a new school only after much discussion at endless town meetings. The high school grades, Connie's particular province, were contained in the older part of the building, the school committee operating on the assumption that older students were less susceptible to drafts and less in need of emergency trips to the newer and handier rest rooms. The new classrooms were more modern, more energy-efficient, more packed to capacity with the expanding numbers of the island's baby boomers' kids. The rooms in the older building were big, high-ceilinged, long-windowed, and the eight junior U.S. history students in front of Connie seemed lost in empty and echoing space.

There had once been nine juniors, of course, and Bentley's absence was one reason why the dynamics were off. But Carlisle Brown's return to school today was another. She sat in the middle of the second row as isolated as if she were alone in the room, surrounded by an aura of . . . Connie didn't know what to call it, but the students around

Carlisle all looked away from her, trying to busy themselves with something or someone in another direction, unable or unwilling or just plain not knowing how, to break through Carlisle's shell. But there was something *else* wrong. Connie was sure of it. What?

Was it that every single pair of eyes that turned from Carlisle failed to light on anyone else? Was it that the silence, something a teacher seldom heard on first entering a classroom, was so complete? Suddenly Connie felt a cold wind of suspicion that the thing that was really bothering these eight students was not Bentley's absence or Carlisle's presence, but the presence of all the rest of them. Someone killed Bentley. Was it someone in this room? Wouldn't they all be thinking that, wondering that? Or *would* they be wondering? What if they *knew?* How easy would it be for someone in this tightly contained little community to kill one of its students without at least one other student knowing *something?*

Connie looked around the room, at the faces she was only just beginning to recognize, and suddenly felt a little bit frightened. Could it be possible that someone in this room killed Bentley? All at once she felt that what she had intended to do with this class today was not going to sit right, not with them, and not with her.

"I'm not going to do any talking today," she began, and immediately someone on the far side of the room said, "Whew!" Connie looked around, expecting, and finding, the short, stocky form topped with white-blond hair that she had already identified, as much as she hated labels, as belonging to the class clown, Alan Anderson. Some rustles and giggles accelerated around the room. Thanks to Alan, some of the tension seemed to have eased. Natalie Price, ordinarily one to attract a male eye by doing nothing more than breathing, was leaning over her sock and trying to push it into just the right slouch, and Alan was watching her do it. Around Carlisle the atmosphere was not much changed, but it seemed to Connie that expressions had softened—Henry Tourville on one side of her no longer seemed to have his mouth locked in a straight line, and Travis Dearborn, on the other, had a less corrugated forehead. Still, the class was not going to chip in and help out much, and Connie knew that she was right in abandoning any further discussion for the day. She about-faced on a squeaky heel and returned to her desk at the front of the room.

"Okay. U.S. history. Today's events. Tomorrow's history. I'd like to take the rest of the class and have you all write something for me. I would like you to think of this day, this year, all the previous years that you have lived, and the years that you will have ahead of you . . ." Connie paused and looked at Carlisle. Her head had been angled stiffly down, but now she was looking steadily at Connie, her face without expression. "And tell me what the history books of the future will have to say about you."

The rustling now became mumbling.

"Any questions?"

There seemed to be a few comments, still mumbled inaudibly, but there were no questions. She looked around the room. Carlisle Brown was staring at her desk again, and Travis Dearborn's pale, fatigued face, and Henry Tourville's pensive one, were watching her. Again, everyone else seemed to shift and look away, not knowing what to do with their eyes or bodies. Connie settled down at her desk and began to do the assignment herself. I will be standing on the beach when the first UFO lands, she wrote. Unfortunately I will be standing on the *exact spot* where it lands. I will not end up in it, I will end up under it, squashed. The marker they erect to commemorate my demise will read: Here landed the first UFO from Uthlot. Here also lies the remains of an unidentified thirty-six-year-old woman who was never missed by anybody. Substituting for her in the junior U.S. history class is a beach ball semiinflated with large quantities of hot air . . .

When Connie looked up, eight faces were staring at her. She stopped smiling.

\* \* \*

39

She was sitting in the one chair in the one sittable room of her apartment, reading over the essays from the history class for the millionth time, when there was a knock on the door. She jumped up, scattering the papers. She wasn't used to visitors here. Not yet. She pounded down the stairs in her socks and opened the door. There stood the one person she probably least expected to see—the chief of police.

"I wonder if you have a minute to talk?"

Connie stared at him. In the brief history of their acquaintance, every time the two of them met, sooner or later one of them was hollering at the other, but as she examined the squinting dark eyes before her, she could find no clues as to the who or why of today's anticipated hollering. "Your place or mine?" she asked him.

He seemed startled. He was a tall, solidly constructed man, often considered to be fat; but Connie, who had a bit of an eye for that kind of thing, was convinced that what everyone else considered excess flab was, in part at least, muscle. His eyes opened wide and then narrowed. He didn't know what the hell she was talking about.

"I mean, are you arresting me, or what?"

"No. Of course not." Now he seemed embarrassed. He pushed a hand through his hair, which was coppishly short and receding, and half grinned at her. "Unless I don't know something I should?"

Connie shrugged that off. "So what do you want?"

He matched the brusqueness of her tone at once. "Answers. To some questions. That I hope I don't have to ask you out here."

She looked at him once more, saw nothing she wasn't supposed to see, turned, and led him up the stairs. Once back in her sitting room, she looked around. There was the one old rocking chair, and the lobster trap that was serving, for now, as a coffee table, and the papers that still lay scattered half on the lobster trap and half on the floor. The chief wasn't looking at them, though, he was looking over her shoulder at the picture that she had just hung on the

40

wall with her brand-new hammer and nails, a watercolor Pete had given her of the creek and the marsh in front of Factotum.

"Nice."

Connie agreed. She waved him toward the one chair, then perched on the corner of the lobster trap and began to scoop up the papers. The chief sat down and began to help, but suddenly he straightened up, frowning at the paper in his hand.

"So give me a hint. I assume you're here about Bentley, but are you here because you think I know something about it or because you think I had something to do with it?"

It took the chief a while, but finally he seemed to register what she had said. He looked up at her and grinned. When he grinned, he really grinned, but not for long—a glimpse of squared-off white teeth and creases from a lot of previous grinning flashed in his face and were gone. "I should think you've got a pretty good alibi for the Saturday in question."

Connie would have blushed if she were a blusher, which she was not. Her face grew a little hotter, that was all.

"I believe," continued the chief, "that on the Saturday in question, for most of the particular time in question, you were standing in front of my desk screaming at me because of a speeding ticket given to you by Paul Roose?"

Connie slapped the papers in her hand down onto the lobster trap. "I wasn't screaming at you for two whole hours. And I had a legitimate—"

The chief raised an opened palm in concession and squinted at her. "Two hours?"

"Between three to five P.M., the time Bentley was killed." She saw the surprise in his face that she would know that. Hadn't he gotten used to this island yet?

The chief made some sort of mental adjustment marked by a quick shake of his head, then raised one of the papers he was holding and snapped it out straight.

"These papers are from which class, Mrs. Bartholomew, the juniors?"

Connie winced at the "Mrs. Bartholomew." She should change her name back, of course, and she kept meaning to do it, but something always got in the way. "Connie, please," she said, and then got worried for a minute that he might think calling her Connie was supposed to mean something. "Yes," she added fast, "the juniors."

"And this particular assignment . . . ?"

" 'What the History Books Will Say About Me.' "

The chief raised his eyebrows, and rows of tanned creases sprang up to his hairline. "Henry Tourville," he read aloud. " 'The history books will refer to me as the genius who invented the GOVUTER, the computer that takes the place of all government officials. Unfortunately, my fame as an inventor will be overshadowed when I murder my wife and her lover with a blowtorch.' "

Connie laughed. "I think I'm going to like him."

The chief looked at her. "Did you happen to notice if Henry was wearing a class ring?"

"A class ring?"

"One was found on the beach where Bentley Brown was killed."

Connie shot up off the lobster trap, and the chief rose with her, towering over her despite Connie's five feet eight inches. It occurred to her that someone who looked like three-quarters of a California Redwood and was a cop to boot should be scary, but for some reason, he wasn't.

"And of course, that's only one of my problems," he continued. "The other is that Bentley Brown was pregnant and no one knows who by. I don't suppose you've been hearing things in the halls?"

Connie glared at him. She felt like taking back the part about calling her Connie. "Is that why you came here? To make me a rat?"

The look the chief gave her was not pleasant, and after a few seconds Connie found she was attempting to explain herself, not something she did very often. "I mean, I don't see why you can't just ask them, ask the kids. What am I supposed to know that they don't?"

The chief continued to study her. "You're a teacher," he said finally. "You know what and how kids get taught. School is a small part of it. At home they learn not to trust anyone from over the causeway. From their friends they learn not to be a rat."

Without extra emphasis he still managed to provide the word "rat" with something that made that hotness return to Connie's face. He looked down at the one remaining paper he still held, and handed it to Connie. "What the history books will say about me," he said.

The paper was completely blank except for the name at the top: Carlisle Brown.

# Chapter
# 5

Sarah Abrew looked through her misty lenses at the man on her couch and felt a physical pain in the middle of her guts. She was old, very old, and she had gained a philosophy late in life as had few of her contemporaries, a philosophy that recognized the ebb and flow of things, a philosophy that acknowledged only the destructive powers of worry, and still, here she sat, looking at the thin, worn shadow of Peter Bartholomew, and feeling this knot in her guts.

There was a day not too long past when she would have tried to fix things, when her main motive in life had been to get Peter and Connie back together, where everyone but they were convinced they belonged, but lately as she watched him read the morning paper, she had come to realize that you can't flow unless first you ebb, and she had settled back to let whatever was going to be, be.

But now this. Now Bentley Brown dead, and Pete looking closer to death with each passing day, and suddenly she was feeling old, frightened, no longer sure that anything was going to "be," for any of them. Pete sighed from the couch, and Sarah, upright and alert again in her chair opposite him, snapped, "What?"

"That's it," he said, looking up at her and smiling with

a smile that he didn't use often enough, as if he didn't want to flaunt his nearly perfect natural teeth in the face of her artificial ones. "End of today's troubles. Didn't take too long today, did it?"

Sarah considered him. He had made no move to get up and get on with his work, and for once she decided to indulge in a whim of the old and alone, to keep this handsome and entertaining young man beside her a little longer. "Bentley's obit should be in today; you're going to read me that, aren't you?"

"No," said Pete, confirming what Sarah had long suspected—a careful censorship at his hands of the daily news.

Sarah adjusted her spindly legs beneath her, released her grip on her cane, and circled the arms of her chair with gnarled fingers. "Yes," she countered. "Read it. Nothing was ever made to go away by the avoiding of it, Peter."

His head snapped up, and even Sarah's fading eyesight could read the suspicion in his once overly trustful brown eyes. He thinks I'm up to my tricks again, she thought, he thinks I'm talking about Connie. Not anymore. At least not this time. I just need to hear it, to hear what the paper has to say about that shadowy girl who came into our lives so unobtrusively, and so flagrantly went out of it. "Read it, Peter," she said, and with a sigh so loaded that she wondered what else he was thinking, he began to read.


Pete was thinking that it was a pretty damned oppressive obit for someone so young and so full of life, and he hated to think that someone, somewhere, felt this was a sufficient summing up. But what would he have added to the mundane reeling off of where she was born, where she went to school, where she died, and who survived her? There wasn't, after all, all that much that he could add, not having known her very well, but couldn't someone else have remembered something special she had done, something worth noting in the last words that would ever be written about her? But no, Pete checked himself; these would not be the last words ever written about her, not once the story was out about what really did happen on the beach—there might be more written about Bentley than anyone really wanted to know. But what could possibly have happened that day? Pete could not imagine Bentley arousing anyone's anger to the extent that that person would kill her, and secretly he still harbored a suspicion of some accidental injury that camouflaged itself as murder on this now overly murder-conscious island. Pete looked once again at the obituary and wondered, had it been Carlisle's, if it would have been much different. Yes, he decided, it would—they would have mentioned that she starred on the volleyball team, they would have mentioned her hilarious rendition of Mrs. Parkhurst in the school play, they would have mentioned her organizing the Fun Club, the club she created just for its stated purpose, and they might have even briefly described some of the events the club had run.

But this was Bentley's obit, and Bentley hadn't been a leader, not even much of a joiner. You couldn't fit things like intensity, sincerity, and intelligence into newspaper obituaries. You couldn't describe feelings like admiration, respect, and plain old affection in print. Pete followed the short paragraph down to its close, gently folded the paper together, and stood up.

"See you tomorrow." He leaned over until his lips brushed the papery skin on Sarah's forehead, and he clasped her warm, nut brown hand. Did she seem to hang on to his a little longer than usual? He bent down again and caught her eyes scanning his face with worry. "Hey! I'm all right! I'll see you tomorrow!"

"Good," said Sarah. It was not the half-irritated blast with which she usually sent him out the door, and as Pete climbed into his old blue truck, his face reflected a goodly portion of her ill-defined anxiety.

The feeling only got worse. As Pete swung the truck off Sarah's road and onto Main Street in the direction of Beston's store, he spotted Connie's Triumph parked in front. What was she doing, becoming one of the porch people? He reversed direction, cut onto Shore Road, and kept driving. The next thing he noticed was the Browns' house, and that didn't exactly help things any. He really should stop in. Carlisle hadn't come back to work, he hadn't seen Ree around. Before he could begin to line up his excuses for not stopping, he pulled the truck in to their drive.

There was a man in the front yard raking leaves out of a circular flower bed, and when he heard Pete's truck, he straightened and turned around. Pete knew Jimmy Solene, and he raised a hand in a wave but was mildly surprised at how unenthusiastic he felt about it. Jimmy Solene had been a couple of grades ahead of Pete in school, and he had been pretty much of a bully then, and Pete had never completely gotten over the feeling that he was still pretty much of a bully now. The fact that Pete had once run into the wrong end of Jimmy Solene's fist didn't improve his opinion of the man any, but it had been a long time ago, and to compensate for this negative feeling, Pete put a little extra something into his wave. Jimmy Solene didn't seem to much care what he put into it—he nodded his head, turned back to the garden, and didn't look around again.

Ree was home alone, and when she opened the door wide enough to recognize him, a smile that Pete had to conclude was fairly forced lit up her eyes.

"Pete!" A battle of some kind was going on behind her eyes. Finally she lurched forward, looped her arm into his, and pulled him into the room. "Come in! You're just the person I feel like seeing right now!" Her voice was unrealistically light, and Pete had some trouble believing it.

"I won't stay, Ree, I just wanted to see how you were, if there was anything I could do . . ."

"Do! You can sit right down here and talk to me! I'll get you a coffee. Sit down!" She was, however falsely, emphatic, and as she spoke, she leaned into him and pushed with the flats of her palms against his chest so that Pete could either stand and struggle or sit and sigh. He chose the latter, but only as long as she was still in the room.

The Brown house was not a house in which Pete felt especially comfortable. The rooms were too open and airy, too cold and gray. Pete stood up and wandered over toward the window. As he neared it, he heard another car approaching. He stood back from the window so that he wouldn't be seen from without, and watched as Carlisle clambered out of Travis Dearborn's father's ancient Olds and tore around the front toward the house. She didn't look happy. No, she wasn't. Travis had leaped out after her, caught up with her midlawn, and grabbed her arm. She pulled away; he lurched and grabbed again. Carlisle's head jerked up and down in what must have been angry bursts of speech. She moved on, he followed until she stopped, and this time her body language, which had seemed clear enough to Pete, finally appeared to be clear enough for Travis. He came no farther. Pete turned away from the window and three things happened simultaneously—Carlisle burst through the front door, Ree returned from the kitchen, and the phone beside the couch began to ring.

Ree picked up the phone. "Hello!" she chirped in the same bright voice. Maybe it isn't just me, thought Pete.

"Hi, Carlisle," said Pete, and Carlisle, her face a storm, managed to muster only enough good grace to pause and acknowledge him.

"Hi, Pete."

"Haven't seen you around, just wanted to see if there was any way I could be useful."

"No, thanks," she said, but she continued to stand and stare at him as if demanding something more from him, something that she considered her due, but what? Pete didn't know, and he thought again of Travis. Poor Travis.

"Not that I expected you back at work," Pete added. "I didn't mean to—"

"Actually," she said, "I haven't wanted to hang around people too much right now."

"Don't blame you," said Pete. "Of course, sometimes being busy helps. We have lots of things to do at Factotum where people aren't, if you feel like filling some time, making some bucks . . ."

Behind him, his ears picked up a very familiar name. "Certainly, Maxine," he heard Ree say.

"No!" said Carlisle, and Pete, who thought she was giving him a definitive answer, turned back to find her waving and shaking her head in a negative at her mother before she bolted up the stairs. "I'll have her call you, Maxine." Ree replaced the receiver and sighed wearily. "Please! Sit and have some coffee." She bent over to the tray she had placed on a coffee table that was too Danish-modern for Pete's taste, and immediately splashed hot coffee all over her hand. "Aah!" She jumped backward into Pete and he grabbed her, his left hand closing around her breast as he came from behind. Mistake! He let go fast. She teetered sideways, shrieking again, her flailing arm catching the handle of the coffee pot as she went down, coffee now covering not only the table but Ree's cream-colored pants and the powder blue rug as well.

Feet pounded on the stairs. "What's going on?" Carlisle demanded. Pete helped Ree up, with more caution this time, and Carlisle ran to the kitchen, returning with a roll of paper towels. Ree began to explain. Pete began to apologize. It was certainly a unique feeling, the feeling of a breast, and it reminded him of how long it had been since he last felt one. Then Ree began to laugh. Pete looked at her. It was a very natural, very nice sound, and he started laughing with her, relieved to see her look like her old self. Then he looked at Carlisle.

Carlisle wasn't laughing. Not cracking a smile. She continued to mop up, her movements rigid, and when Pete turned back to face Ree again, he saw that she was staring at Carlisle too. With only the slightest variation in pitch, Ree stopped laughing and began to cry.

They hadn't seemed to want him there after that, if they had ever wanted him there in the first place, and remembering it, Pete was surprised that afternoon when he finally returned to Factotum, after having planted about a hundred tulip bulbs for the Whiteaker Hotel, to find two messages

being waved at him from between Rita's glossy red nails—
one from Ree, and one from Ree's daughter.

Pete picked the note out of Rita's fingers. "Dinner," said
the one from Ree. "Seven P.M. Sunday. R.S.V.P. by 6:55.
Carlisle out." Did she mean the part about Carlisle to be
inducement or threat? And why? Maybe she wanted to talk
to him about Carlisle? That was, after all, the only interpretation that made sense.

The second message was less cryptic. "Carlisle wants to
come back to work," it said. "Will stop by Monday after
school."

"Thanks, Rita," said Pete, and still looking at the notes,
he began to walk in the direction of the hall.

"*Wait* a minute, here!" Rita's heels clicked mutely after
him over the soft pine floor. "What is this, a date?"

"Of course not," said Pete, fighting off two images: one,
an old one, of past and futile attempts by Rita to get him
to forget about Connie in the arms of another woman, any
woman, and a second, extremely adolescent one, of actually *seeing* the breast he had previously only felt.

"Right," said Rita in the way only Rita could say
"right," which was, if you came right down to it, in this
particular instance at least, all wrong. It was not a date.
Ree Brown didn't even particularly like him. For one thing,
why had she hired Jimmy Solene to do her yard, Jimmy
who was not known as the most reliable person on Nashtoba by any means, while if there was one thing everyone
knew about Factotum, it was that they were reliable? And
reasonable. And Pete had never hit anybody in his *life*.

Rita Peck looked at her watch for the sixth time in five
minutes and decided to treat herself to the unaccustomed
luxury of unleashed anger. She jabbed off the light switch
over her desk and slammed the file drawer shut with the
heel of her shoe. Where was that darned kid? For once in
her life, couldn't she be where she was supposed to be at
the time she was supposed to be there? Was Rita asking
too much? She didn't think so. She opened the front door

of Factotum, and just as she did, the phone began to ring. She stalked over to it, picked it up, and said rather forcefully, she knew, "Factotum!"

"Whew! Sweetie! Don't tell me you're sounding a wee touch miffed! Not you! Not my little angel! Is Pete there?"

Rita groaned. It was Bert Barker. "No, Bert."

"No? Well, what's his friend at the cop shop say these days? Any big arrest pending? Pete's in on it, I know."

"Only because he found her. That's as in on it as he wants to get. Now I have to—"

"What, hasn't he sniffed out any clues?"

Rita decided to resort to her old standard: the white lie. "Oh!" she exclaimed. "Someone's at the door! Good-bye, Bert!" and she dumped the phone. Someone *was* at the door, she consoled herself, and not seconds later—herself. She looked out, then walked around the corner and looked out over the marsh to the beach, but she couldn't see anyone on the beach at all, certainly not the form of her overdue daughter. What she did see, however, was a metallic tinge in the sky that told her it was not long before the sun would be gone, and although at first it reminded her of the lateness of her daughter and did nothing but deepen her displeasure, after a minute and three deep breaths of revitalizing September air, she took another look and thought of other things. It was peaceful out here. The marsh was every color of no color, the beach glinted and gleamed, the water was whispering and calm, and suddenly Rita needed to be near it. She sat down on Pete's typically prickly and sparse Nashtoba lawn, kicked off her shoes, peeled off her stockings, left them on his front step, and stretched out her long-unused legs in the direction of the cooling sand.

With each step she could almost feel some particle of worry slide from her shoulders onto the ground. Where was Maxine? Where she always was, at the Shack, with friends, and if she wasn't here at Factotum in time for Rita to drive her home, she would have to get a ride from one of them and deal with the consequences later; there was nothing else Rita could do about it now.

And who would Rita get to do Peale's garage? Despite what Pete said, Rita knew by reading his eyes that he was nowhere near ready for that kind of strenuous work; so it was time to hire someone else.

And what about her own life? How much of her anger with Maxine stemmed from jealousy, jealousy that Maxine would race home now only to go out again later with friends, while Rita would be stretching out alone on the couch with a book? She tossed her head and looked up, and there, much farther down the beach than she should have been by now, was Maxine.

And not alone. The person walking next to her was turning away, walking back toward the marsh, but Maxine was following. The figure stopped, turned, hovered, turned away again, began to walk again, was followed by Maxine again, stopped again . . .

Rita continued to walk toward them, determined, today, not to cut short her own pleasure just to give her daughter more space. As Rita got closer, she recognized the tall form beside Maxine. He was not hard to spot—the awkwardness of the situation could not camouflage the natural grace of the school's best athlete, and the filtered sun only threw his dark hair and striking profile into greater relief. The body language was also clear to read—the attempts by Travis Dearborn to pull away, the puppy-dog insistence on Maxine's part to follow, made Rita feel ashamed for her daughter, but it was only Maxine's sighting of her mother down the beach that made the tableau change.

First it froze. Maxine, then Travis, stared toward her, and somehow, in some subtle fashion, everything seemed to reverse itself as if in a mirror. Now Travis leaned toward Maxine, a hand on her shoulder, walking along with her, leading her, it seemed; and Maxine now drew away from the helping hand. They proceeded in this balky fashion some feet, then Travis hung back and Maxine came on alone.

"What are you doing with that Travis?" Rita asked, and

heard her own voice and at once knew she had done it again. That Travis.

Maxine didn't answer her. They walked, in silence, back up the beach and over the marsh to Factotum and the car.

When they got home, Maxine went upstairs at once.

"Dinner in half an hour!" Rita yelled up the stairs. She was so tired of yelling.

"Not hungry!" Maxine yelled down.

"Maxine," Rita began, attempting to make her voice sound calm at high decibels, something not that easy to accomplish, "you have *got* to—"

"I ate at the Shack!"

Yes, but *what*? wondered Rita. And in how many minutes would who-knows-who-else be picking you up to return there?

Rita wondered why it was that despite their deteriorating relationship, she was never once *glad* that Maxine was going out and leaving her alone. Was it the aloneness? Or was it her constant and ever-changing set of worries about cars with sixteen- and seventeen-year-olds behind the wheel, the incessant intakes of empty calories with no protein, no vegetables, no *fruit* . . .

No, Rita decided. It wasn't any of that exactly, or maybe it was all of that. The little creep, the monster in costly clothes, was still the object of all her deepest feelings of love, and even these fleeting glimpses of her as she ran up the stairs and down the stairs and out the door and into cars were better than no glimpses, were better than a life without her, were better than . . . All of a sudden Rita thought of Bentley Brown, and of how fragile life really was, and she felt her knees give way beneath her. She sat down on the bottom stair, her eyes full of tears. Rita was never one to waste tears, and these soon became multipurpose—tears for Bentley, tears for Ree, tears for herself, tears for her own daughter, Maxine, who had had to go through this all firsthand. Of course, that was the explanation for a lot of it, wasn't it? Hadn't Maxine been suffering under the strain of Bentley's death? Rita pulled herself up by the banister, all at once full of purpose. She marched up the stairs to Maxine's door and knocked, hard.

"What."

Rita pushed open the door, and Maxine, who had been lying crosswise on her bed with her head and arms hanging down, immediately jumped up. "What!" she snapped again.

Rita looked at her in silence for some minutes. She had marched up here to offer her love to her daughter, to explain, yet again, that she was here if she needed her, and after taking one look at her daughter's face, she knew that that was the last thing that Maxine needed to hear just then. "Before you go anywhere tonight," she said, her voice as hard as she could make it, "you are going to eat a *normal* meal in a *normal* house at a *normal* hour. Do you understand?"

Maxine resumed her previous pose, but not before she muttered a sound that Rita recognized as scornful acquiescence.

Rita decided to take that grudging response as enough of a gift for one night and went downstairs, suspecting that her own hard words had after all been that very message of love she had intended. She went into the kitchen and began to fuss around with dinner, suddenly feeling better, less daunted by the prospect of Saturday night. Maybe she would call Pete, see if he felt like coming over again, not that he was exactly the liveliest of company these days . . . The phone rang at Factotum a long time, but no one answered.

Pete sipped at his beer and looked sideways at Willy McOwat, trying to remember a time when his Saturday night companion at Lupo's had been someone else, preferably a woman, preferably one particular woman, and thinking, instead, of one particular Saturday night that he and Connie had spent at home alone.

"Quiet, you say," Willy asked him, for at least the third time.

"Quiet," Pete answered.

"Morose, would you say?"

Pete considered the word *morose* as an adjective describing Bentley Brown. "Not morose," he answered. "Quiet. Maybe a little moodier of late, now that I think about it."

"Popular?"

"No," Pete answered so decisively that Willy looked at him in surprise. "Well, not as much as Carlisle. Carlisle is pretty big-time stuff, I'd say."

"Boyfriends?"

"None to my knowledge. I never saw her with anyone except her sister and her sister's crowd." Wasn't it odd, thought Pete, that he would call it her sister's crowd?

"Best friends?"

"No, we weren't," said Pete, becoming tired of answering questions.

"No best friend, no boyfriend, you tell me she wouldn't have been wearing a boy's ring, you don't know whose ring might have been on the beach that day attached to whose finger . . ."

"For God's sake," said Pete, "I hardly knew the girl. Ask someone who knew her."

"Like who?"

"Who?" Pete repeated. "Her mother, her sister, or . . ."

"Or?"

Pete looked into the bottom of his beer, remembered that Willy was driving, and waved at the bartender for another. "All I know about Bentley Brown," said Pete, "is that she was a spring," and he proceeded to explain at length about spring. Willy didn't seem to be half as bored as Pete had expected him to be, and the conversation about colors went on a good two beers longer. Pete, who in the past had never been much of a drinker, seemed to be developing a certain skill at being a barfly. Well, where else was there to go when you didn't want to be at home alone?

\* \* \*

Perhaps that was why, when Ree threaded her hand through his and pulled him inside the next evening, it felt pretty good. She looked pretty good, too. She was wearing a corduroy skirt that was tight enough to require a slit up the back, and a sweater that was just loose enough to swing when she did. Almost at once she handed him a drink of something colorless in a stemmed glass, which would have looked like a martini had it held anything else, such as an olive.

"Carlisle is out," she whispered, as if Carlisle were really still in. "It was touch and go for a minute, I tell you, something about Travis having forgotten all about some play, trying to beg off the whole thing. You don't do that to Carlisle and not expect a few words to fly! So he came, late, I might tell you, but he came, and I can't hide my delight at being able to sit down and have a drink and talk to you like this alone!" As she spoke, she dropped abruptly onto the sofa so that Pete, still attached to her by one hand, was forced to fall down beside her, sloshing his drink all over his white cotton shirt. Was everything in this house always spilled? Pete dashed a hand across the larger droplets, but Ree didn't seem to notice.

"I tell you," she went on, "it has certainly been quite some time since the two of us have had a really nice talk."

Pete, who couldn't remember ever having had a really nice talk in the first place, began to feel a little puzzled. He leaned forward to place his drink on the coffee table, and as he did so, he moved himself a fraction over to the right, to give them both a little room.

"I saw your friend this morning," said Ree. She leaned forward to pick up her own colorless drink, and somehow managed to situate herself so that they once again sat thigh to thigh. "He says you sent him back here?"

If Pete hadn't already figured out who she meant by her words, he would have been able to do so by her tone—the new chief might have been doing his damnedest to figure out who had killed Ree's daughter, but she still didn't like him any more than the other islanders did.

"He was asking me about Bentley," said Pete. "I'm sorry if he disturbed you in any way, but I really did not feel expert enough to comment on Bentley's friends. I suggested that he talk to you or Carlisle again instead." Pete reached forward for his drink and took a taste. The one taste required another right after it to make sure he was getting it right—he was. Straight gin. Warm. Pete put his drink down, turned to face Ree more directly, and cleared his throat. "I feel like I only knew Bentley well enough to miss her. I—"

Ree covered his hand with cold fingers, shaking her head at him, her eyes full of never-too-distant tears. She shook her head. "Please."

Fair enough. Pete cast around for a new subject, feeling very much as if he *were* on a date, and never having been too adept at it the first time around, he found it much the same all these years later. "Travis seems like a nice guy," he finally contributed, and meager though the contribution was, it seemed to suffice.

"He's lovely," said Ree. "Quite the little star—basketball, soccer, track . . ." She leaned forward to grasp her drink, but she didn't drink from it, she just held on to it. "Carlisle, of course, seems to take it all as her due." She seemed to consider saying something else, discarded it, reclaimed it. "Bentley was so different," she said, in a voice that was harder, strange in some ways. "The type that Bentley went for was that Coke-bottle-lens type." She looked at Pete, seeming suddenly nervous. "She was pregnant. I suppose you know that. I think that must explain her behavior of late. She was so snappish, not like herself at all, she actually set to with Carlisle over a piece of *toast* the other day, it just wasn't like her. Carlisle can be a little . . ." Ree seemed to give a half-guilty start at whatever it was that she had been going to say about her one remaining daughter. She changed her tack. "Bentley had always been so . . . so . . . patient with Carlisle, able to take in her stride the sometimes thoughtless things that . . ." Again, Ree backed off. "Anyway, I suppose once that chief gets through, everyone is going to know Bentley was pregnant, not that I care, really, not in this day and age, of course."

But Pete got the strong feeling that she *did* care, and cared very much. She jumped up then, upsetting, for the second time, the drink that Pete had just raised to his lips. Most of the rest of it went down his throat in a burning wave, with just enough left out to dribble over his chin. Ree looked down at him in surprise as she passed.

"Why, I think you need another."

Pete didn't feel like drinking, or wearing, another, and he clung to his glass. Ree's glass, he noticed, was nearly untouched and miraculously still full. By the time they moved on to the table for dinner, Pete realized he had best go easy on the wine he had brought—it seemed to him that she kept touching him, and he knew it couldn't be on purpose, but still, it made him think along the lines of keeping a clear head. He concentrated on eating deliciously rare roast beef and answering a lot of questions.

"How did you get to be so friendly with this chief? Was it because you helped him before?"

Pete answered yes to that one.

"And does he tell you all his findings?" The word "findings" seemed to be loaded with sarcasm—Pete settled for a negative nod and a mouthful of baked potato on that.

"And just who does he think killed my daughter?" asked Ree, and the baked potato turned left instead of right somewhere halfway down and ended up lodged in his windpipe. A great deal of coughing, wine, and hands-on sympathy later, Pete looked up with bleary eyes to see two very clear ones still waiting for an answer.

"I have no idea," said Pete, and tried to look at his watch before he remembered he wasn't wearing one, which was just as well, since a lot of gin had sloshed over his wrist of late.

"Well then, who do you think killed her?" Ree stood up

and moved behind Pete, resting one hand on his shoulder and reaching around him with the other for his empty plate so that he couldn't see her face, and couldn't say for sure if the brittle detachment in her voice was for real.

Pete stood up, pushed back his chair, and took the plates out of her hands, partly because he wanted to help and partly because he didn't feel like wearing roast beef juice on his shirt as well.

"I think whatever happened out there on the beach was an accident," he said. "I don't think anyone on this island hated Bentley, could have hated Bentley enough to mean to harm her. I think it's hard enough to have lost a daughter without having to be thinking about some kind of hate having taken her. I don't think anyone meant to do it, Ree."

"But *who?*" said Ree. She had followed him into the kitchen. Pete put down the plates and turned around to find her very close to him.

"I have no idea," he answered. All at once she seemed extremely drunk, drunker than the little alcohol he had seen her consume would explain, and Pete remembered the prescription Hardy had given her and began to wonder if she had taken some tranquilizers. She swayed against him. Pete folded his arms around her, and she burrowed into him as if she were cold. Was that it? Was it just a hug that she needed? Her arms were around him, and her fingers were holding on to his back belt loops as if for dear life.

"I've always liked you, Pete," she said into his neck. "I've always figured you for a real nice guy."

And just what, wondered Pete, did a real nice guy do now? He turned his head just enough sideways to catch sight of the dirty dishes piled beside the sink, and Ree Brown bit him on the ear.

# Chapter
# 6

Maxine Peck stared at the top of her head in the mirror over the bathroom sink, saw the two girls behind her file out through the door for the next class, and decided to regel her hair. She finished pulling her hair up into spikes, washed the gunk off her fingers, and looked at her watch. She decided it was really too late to bother showing up at class at all—if she walked in now, her teacher would have things to say about it, and Maxine was tired of hearing people say things about things. She decided to stay there in the bathroom and write a note to Travis. *That Travis*. So her mother didn't like him! Somehow since that remark of her mother's, Maxine had been able to focus more clearly on all the great things about him, and he was becoming bigger and better and more special, her feelings about him all the more important the more they differed from her mother's. *That Travis*. Right now she needed to see him, to talk to him, but Travis wasn't the easiest person to get close to these days.

Maxine looked at herself once again in the mirror and frowned. She wished she didn't look so . . . so . . . fifteen. She was really too goo-goo-eyed, that was the whole problem—no matter what she tried to do to herself, she had these big brown eyes that popped wide open all the time and made her look like she had never even *heard* of the word condom. No wonder Travis didn't seem interested in talking to her. And really, that was all she wanted to do, talk to him. Of course, she would never try to steal him away from Carlisle, not that she *could* steal him away from Carlisle, but Carlisle was getting pretty arrogant about Travis, after all, acting like she automatically deserved him all the time, treating him like he was supposed to bow down when he was around her or something. Travis might get pretty tired of that, not that she *really* wished he would, not really, especially not now that Carlisle's sister was dead . . . Maxine felt again that lurching of her stomach as it rose up into her throat whenever she thought about Bentley, saw that image of Bentley, gray-white in the water with her eyes half open and the gaudy streak of shadow on the lids . . . She ran for the stall and vomited loudly. She felt horrible. Should she go see the nurse? No. The nurse was one of those "I'm calling your mother this minute!" types, and if she called her mother, her mother would think she was pregnant or on drugs or whatever it was she was reading about this week in those magazines over the top of which she kept peering at Maxine, watching and waiting.

Maxine washed her face, careful not to splash her hair, unwrapped a piece of gum, and tried to figure out how she could manage to run into Travis as he came out of gym class and headed for Connie Bartholomew's history class and still make it to her own English class on the second floor on time. She decided to go to the gym doors and hang out there until the bell, and then race like mad back up the stairs once she had said a word or two to Travis, but it must have been later than she thought. The bell rang before she had even reached the gym, and she had to scan faces fast, looking for him in the hall.

As Maxine looked at her fellow students' faces, she saw things in them that had not been there a short time before. It was all because of Bentley, Maxine knew, but still, she didn't quite understand it. *Some* of it she could understand, of course, could understand as she passed Carlisle that she should look like the walking dead, not saying hi to Maxine at all, but what was with Henry Tourville, for instance? He was not Carlisle's type *at all*, not nerdy Henry, with his way of talking that made you have to stop to figure it all out, his clever conversation that left you thinking there was more of a joke than you were getting first time out. He was okay-looking, she guessed, if you liked glasses and tall, skinny types who had broad, bony shoulders and serious faces. Here he was, walking beside Carlisle looking like he was her secret service agent, as if some maniac were out there trying to kill all the twins. He was walking right next to Carlisle, right where Travis should be, as a matter of fact, but Travis was nowhere to be seen. And Anna Pease, looking all around for Travis, Maxine could bet. And where *was* Travis? But there he came now, looking ahead, right through Maxine; he didn't seem to see whatever it was he wanted to see, or else saw what it was that he didn't want to see. In that long, graceful lope of his that made Maxine feel like crying, he wove his way through the hall and out of sight.

Connie couldn't seem to get the image of flashing class rings out of her mind. There were, among the eight juniors in Carlisle Brown's class, four boys and four girls, and of the four boys, three of them were not wearing class rings. *Three* of them. Three of her students had no class rings, and was Connie now supposed to assume that one of those three rings was sitting in a desk drawer at the police station? She felt a sudden fury with the chief as she looked from one of those three faces to the other—did the chief think that she was supposed to just waltz right up to those particular three students and ask them what the hell happened to their rings? And while she was at it, ask them if they had impregnated Bentley?

"Okay," said Connie. "Henry." Henry Tourville took his eyes off Carlisle with reluctance and looked at his teacher. Connie looked at his hand. "It's 1770. You have this real thing about England. It's gotten to be kind of a

personal thing with you, and you think it would be great if
you could engineer some kind of a deal where the colonies
are able to get rid of England altogether, but you've got
this problem. Not everybody feels about England exactly
the way you do. A third of the population of the colonies,
as a matter of fact, is dead set against these ideas of yours.
Another third is on the fence. You've only got one-third
you can really count as with you. What do you do?''

Henry pushed his glasses up on his nose with a ringless
hand, folded his arms, and hunched his upper torso.
"Well," he said. He was soft-spoken, but not tentative. "I
would have to consider the third against as a write-off, I
suspect. If I could do something about convincing the third
on the fence, that should be enough, however."

"And how would you do that?"

"The same way Sam Adams did. I'd lie."

A few laughs, but not as many as Alan, the clown, would
have gotten had he said the same thing, and Connie felt
herself frowning. Didn't Henry mind this? Didn't it just
about kill him that he could twist himself inside out and
still not come out ahead?

"But what if this were today? What advantages and disad-
vantages would you have that Sam didn't? Marty."

"Whew!" Marty was always very taxed by these hypo-
thetical questions. He clutched the edge of his desk, his
hand also ringless, and pushed an unstylishly Beatlesque
bang straight back across the top of his head. "Wow. Gee.
I dunno. Yeah. Dunno."

Marty didn't seem to be much interested in girls, Connie
mused, as Natalie Price leaned over beside him with her
neckline gaping and he didn't so much as swivel one hair
to have a look. Somehow it didn't seem to Connie that
someone not much interested in girls would be apt to beat
one's head in, but still she watched Marty's face return to
its normal sullen state and wondered. Not a happy camper,
Marty. But who could blame him? This was his second
shot at junior year, and try number two wasn't going much
better than the first.

"But how? Anna Pease. How, today, would you attempt to sway public opinion?"

Anna Pease flew back from some private world of her own that must have been light-years away from U.S. history and looked, at once, at Travis Dearborn. She spent most of her conscious moments, which were few and far between, looking at Travis Dearborn, and Connie sighed. It was hard not to look at Travis, not to admire the perfection of his profile and the long, broad back that pulled at his shirt, but just once she wished she could catch one of the girls staring at someone else, someone like Henry Tourville, for instance. True, he was partially hidden behind those grossly magnifying lenses, and he talked like a museum guide half the time, but behind all that was something intriguing and secretive and deep. Connie watched him watching Carlisle Brown and sighed. Carlisle was not for Henry, if only Henry knew. She looked around the room for some other eyes that might not be so blinded by brawn, some eyes that might appreciate the fact that although Henry didn't look like he could get a ball through a hoop if it were sitting in his lap, he *could* get good grades. And Connie had a feeling that Henry's good grades had been achieved with one brain tied behind his back, so to speak, that if he were really interested, he could do great things, could indeed invent the GOVUTER. And could he blowtorch his wife? Connie looked sideways at Carlisle as they all waited an inordinately long time for Anna Pease to decide to admit she had no idea what they were talking about. *Was* Carlisle really and truly as nuts about Travis as the rest of them, or was she just bound and determined to claim the school prize as her own just desserts? Carlisle and Travis were far and away the two most popular students in the school, and if that weren't enough to make them compatible, Connie had also taken the time to look into her students' records and had found that Carlisle and Travis seemed to have similar low priorities when it came to school. Bentley, on the other hand, had done much better in school.

Connie gave up waiting for Anna and switched her attention to Alan Anderson, picking him, she knew, because the third pair of ringless hands was somehow drawing her like a magnet. Alan was smart enough. Unfortunately, Alan was at present only interested in being clever, which was not, as Connie well knew, the same thing.

"Alan," said Connie, "if you were Sam Adams today, what would you do?"

"Start a brewery," said Alan. Waves of laughter rocked through the rows, and Connie found herself feeling a sense of gratitude for the spark Alan had in one swift move returned to the class. Only Henry wasn't smiling. So he minded not getting the laughs. His eyes, blinking behind his glasses, took on a new cast that was not attractive, not heartwarming, no.

Connie struggled onward toward the bell. She resisted stopping Marty Sunderland as he went by to ask if he had ever owned a ring, swearing she could see a band of pale skin on the ring finger of his left hand, resisted again when Alan winked at her on his way out.

Travis pushed ahead of Natalie Price and exited alone, followed in a trail by Anna Pease and Kate McLellan, a plump and pasty girl who was destined to always be last. But no, Kate wasn't last today—Henry Tourville and Carlisle Brown were the last two out of the room, and Connie didn't stop to think about why it was she left hot on their heels, or why it was she pressed forward as they wound their way through the slalom of the corridor until she was within hearing distance of the pair. They seemed to have a lot to say to each other, and Connie caught very little of it, at first.

". . . Factotum today," Carlisle was saying. "I wasn't going to, but I can't just hang around home. Trav's got practice every day now anyway."

"I think you should," said Henry, and he edged her ever so slightly sideways with his arm, skillfully moving her past a senior who was attempting to stop her for a word. Connie noticed that Carlisle took time out from cataloging her woes to flash a grateful smile at the senior, while not forgetting one for Henry.

"I envy you," Henry was saying. "I have often wished I had an after-school source of supplemental funds."

Carlisle stopped and looked up, way up, at Henry, forcing Connie to circle past. "Why don't you come with me? We could ask Pete. Mrs. Peck says he needs tons more help, and she asked Travis, but he couldn't because of all the practices. Why don't you?"

Connie was moving ahead too fast to hear any more, so when she saw the gym teacher, Roy Millis, approaching from the other direction, she raised a hand in greeting, effectively stopping him in his tracks, and consequently giving her a chance to stop also.

"The lovely Mrs. Bartholomew," said Roy Millis, bending at the waist in a mock bow that Connie found as irritating as his form of address. "And how I hoped I might meet you just this way!"

Connie looked at the top of his sandy hair and the pink scalp winking underneath it as he straightened up. He had blue eyes that seemed always red-rimmed, as if he had overindulged in either alcohol or emotion the night before. He was not quite as tall as Connie, and he stretched and fidgeted around her, obviously uncomfortable with their relative distances from the ceiling.

"Roy," said Connie. Henry and Carlisle pulled even with them, talking rapidly, and then moved past.

"Good-bye, Roy," said Connie, moving after her students.

"Hey!" Roy trotted in her wake. "Wait, wait, wait! We have things to discuss! Drinks! Dinner! Drinks again! Then who knows where love will take us?"

Carlisle turned around and stared at Roy Millis, her face a mask of disgust; Roy's lecherous routine wasn't going over well with any generation these days, it appeared.

"Can't," said Connie, intending no further explanation, intending to push ahead after Henry and Carlisle, but Roy hung tight.

"Tomorrow, then. What could you possibly be doing on

a Tuesday? I, on the other hand, will have to break at least fourteen most interesting engagements, and all because of you, but don't give it a second—"

He was walking backward in front of her now, slowing her down and causing her to lose her quarry. God*damn* the man! "Okay!" Connie hollered, pushing past him and breaking into a trot. She peered down the ancient corridor walled with beaten-up lockers and at present very few students. Carlisle and Henry were not among them.

*Damn,* she said to herself. But it served her right, she knew. She was spying. And for what? Or for whom?

# Chapter
7

Pete was exhausted. First of all, there was the fact that he had not gotten much sleep the night before, not that he had done anything much exciting in its place. Soon after Ree Brown had attacked his ear, she had collapsed, and Pete had spent close to two hours trying to pick her up and put her back together, literally and figuratively. In the end he had been forced to call Hardy Rogers, who wasn't much pleased to be shaken out at eleven-thirty at night, but who, once he arrived, was able to sort out wrong from right medications, to leave them with specific and helpful instructions, and to send Pete home. By the time Pete had gotten back, it had been close to 2:00 A.M., and he had lain awake for some time after that, worrying about the Browns.

Add to that the fact that he had already today hauled two boats out of the water and mowed three lawns. Add to *that* the fact that he had to pass by Rita's desk at least twelve times and watch her gaze speculatively at the dark circles under his eyes, add to that that Bert Barker seemed to be spending most of the day hanging around Rita's desk trying to get Pete to stop and gossip.

And then the kids arrived on the school bus. Pete was just coming back from the third lawn as they trooped up to Factotum's steps together: Maxine, Carlisle, and Henry Tourville, the tall boy he had seen at the Browns' house.

"How do you do," Henry said solemnly, and held out a hand to Pete, who, accustomed to Maxine's form of address, found the gesture a bit disconcerting. Or was it something else? Henry reminded him of someone. Pete shook Henry's hand, and noticed that he was not wearing a ring.

"I believe I should have called first, but Carlisle suggested that I come along with her. It would be in regard to a job. She seemed to feel—"

"Mrs. Peck spoke to Travis about it," interrupted Carlisle, "but Travis wasn't interested." Something in her voice indicated that Travis had, with that lack of interest, made a very big mistake in Carlisle's book. "Then I thought of Henry. Mrs. Peck says you need someone because . . ." Whatever reason Mrs. Peck had given, Carlisle seemed to conclude that Pete wasn't going to like it. She didn't finish her thought.

"Well," said Pete, "suppose we all go inside and find out just what Mrs. Peck has in mind." It had always amused him greatly that Rita was Mrs. Peck, while he was plain old Pete, but he figured it had something to do with Rita being older and the mother of a fellow student, and Pete being . . . just Pete.

Rita began giving Henry her usual this-is-Factotum spiel, but Pete wasn't listening. He was mentally measuring his own finger, on which the lost ring had fit fairly well, against Henry's bare one, and concluding that it could fit there as well. But maybe Henry had never ordered a ring. Pete became aware that Rita was frowning at him and Carlisle was staring. He cleared his throat and picked up a note for him on the desk. It was from Ree Brown. "Please call," it said.

"Well?" Rita asked him. "Okay?"

Pete couldn't for the life of him recall what the question had been in the first place, but he didn't feel like appearing as disorganized as he felt.

"Okay," he answered.

"Okay, Henry," smiled Rita, pleased. "You're hired!

Come right this way! Maxine, I could use your help as well." It was not put in the form of a question, and Maxine, who seemed to respond better when she felt she had no choice, followed her mother and Henry out of the room, leaving Pete and Carlisle alone.

"You've been talking to the chief," Carlisle said. "Do you know who killed my sister?"

Pete looked hard at Carlisle's expression and didn't much like what he saw. "No, I don't," he answered. "There are a few things he's working on . . ."

"My sister was pregnant. I didn't know that. Did you know that?"

"No," Pete replied.

"My mother didn't know it either. Not that that surprises me. My mother is the original prude, she would have killed her if she knew."

Pete didn't say anything, but he had begun to develop the strong suspicion that Ree Brown was not exactly what he would have called a prude.

"My sister told me everything. Everything. We were together all the time. I knew where she was all the time. At least I used to . . . She wasn't . . ." Carlisle shook her head, and the red curls quivered. She changed the subject. Sort of. "And you found a ring. I don't know whose it is. Do you? Does *he*?"

He? Willy? Pete shook his head.

"Henry's ring was stolen." Carlisle waited for Pete to register this fact, scanning his face, and Pete watched her do it, scanning hers back, knowing as he did so that she was probably learning a lot more from his than he was from hers. But for some reason Pete suddenly remembered just who it was Henry reminded him of: Glen Newcomb! Glen Newcomb, the guy who had stolen his wife, or, to be more accurate, more painfully accurate, the guy that Connie had stolen from *his* wife.

"He told you this?"

Carlisle nodded. "It happened last Wednesday. He was in the gym working out; he left it in his locker, and when

70

he came back to change, it was gone. Anyone could have taken it. You can open those lockers with a screwdriver—Nat Weams jammed a screwdriver into the crack where the lock is and opened up a whole bunch last year and got kicked out of school for it.''

"Oh," said Pete. It was the best he could do at the moment. If Henry's ring had been stolen, if Henry was indeed telling the truth, did that mean it could have been anyone's ring on the beach? Anyone who, having realized it was gone, having heard, as Carlisle had obviously heard, that one had been found, then went out and stole a replacement . . . assuming, of course, that Henry Tourville was telling the truth, that he was going to the gym to work out . . . And that, alone, Pete found hard to believe, that the tall, skinny Henry had ever worked out. But unathletic as Henry seemed, Pete had little or no trouble believing that Carlisle could find him attractive. He knew from personal experience that those Glen Newcomb types could do a real number on some.

"Did all the juniors order rings?"

Carlisle shrugged and turned away to look out the window. "Something was wrong with my sister," she said. "I know something was wrong with her. She wouldn't come to the games or the Shack anymore. I'd get home and she'd be off, gone. She used to be right *there* all the time . . ." There was something frighteningly flat about Carlisle's voice, her face, even her clothes. Her spark was missing.

The telephone on Rita's desk rang. Pete picked it up, and Carlisle moved toward the door.

"It's me. Ree. I'm calling to apologize for last night and to attempt to make it up to you. I'm all right now, really, and I wondered if you wanted to try again. Any night you want, but Car is going to a game on Tuesday, so that would really be the best night for me. Not that I don't want her around, but sometimes it's less confusing talking adult to adult, do you know what I mean?"

"Yes," Pete lied, having found of late that his conversations with adults were a lot more puzzling than his conversations with teenagers.

"Great!" said Ree. "Tuesday then? Do you like Mexican food? I make terrific enchiladas."

"Great," said Pete, feeling he had somewhere very recently lost complete control of his vocabulary, as well as his life.

"*Great,*" said Ree again, sounding as if she really meant it. Pete couldn't understand it. He hung up the phone, confused. When Rita came in, alone, she took one look at his face and said, "What now?"

Pete suddenly knew exactly "what now." He turned around, shut the door behind Rita, took the phone off the hook, and sat down on his usual spot on the desk in front her. "What's all this about Connie doing all these jobs for us?" he asked her. This time she told him. She tried hard to make it sound like something other than what it was, but what it was was just plain nice, and it finally explained how Factotum had managed to stay afloat with half its work force out of commission.

Physically tired though he was by the time Rita and Maxine and Carlisle and Henry had all gone home, Pete was restless. His side throbbed, his eyes burned, and for the first time in his life, his lower back was aching. He knew he should get something to eat, take a hot shower, and sack out, so he pulled some cold ham, lettuce, and tomato out of the fridge, split open a roll and stuffed it full, then opened a beer and went out onto his porch. The sun had just passed from the deep blue part of the sky into the layer of gray fog on the horizon, and darts of gold were shooting upward through it, as well as downward onto the water below. Pete sat down in the rocker and ate his meal and let the sunset allay his restlessness. The salt hay on the marsh turned from blackish brown to topaz and the creek became liquid light as the sun dropped through the fog, and then the marsh was a black void once again as the sun drained into the sea. Pete continued to sit there, but now that the sun was gone, his restlessness was returning.

There were things to do. He should pass on this new information about Henry Tourville's ring to the chief, of course, so that he could check to see if Henry Tourville's locker had been jimmied as Carlisle had described. That would be the first thing for the chief to do, of course, go to the high school and . . . The high school. And then Pete found he was no longer thinking about the chief at all, but about Connie, and then all of a sudden Pete knew what *he* should be doing: he should be going to see Connie, to thank her for her help over the summer. That was all, just to thank her. It wasn't as if he would be meaning anything by it, it was the courteous thing to do, after all . . .

He jumped up out of the rocking chair so hard and fast that his back locked halfway up and he twisted sideways and yelped at the jab of pain in his ribs. What a mess he was! He threw his empty beer can into the returnable bottle basket, put his plate unwashed in the sink, ran his fingers through his hair without looking at his own telltale eyes in the mirror, and headed for the door.

Connie. Pete pushed aside the debris on the front seat of his old jeep truck and cranked over the engine. For once the truck started without interruption, and Pete found himself sailing smoothly down the narrow lane that led to Shore Road and from there to Coolidge's, where he had heard, had been told discreetly by about sixty different people, that Connie was staying. He looked at the seat beside him and saw that the donut bag from Mable's was still crumpled up on it, and remembered about Mable's sign.

Pete slowed the truck. What did he think he was doing? Didn't everyone keep telling him that Connie had not wanted him to know she had helped out? And why? So that he wouldn't do exactly what he was doing right now, so that he wouldn't go see her. He slammed on his brakes and backed and turned and backed and turned until he was heading the other way on the narrow road.

If Connie had meant anything by helping out, she would

have made damned sure Pete knew all about it. Subterfuge was not one of Connie's strong suits, and if she had decided to become devious, then it was because there was something at stake. Obviously she didn't want to see him, and Pete, feeling foolish that he had ever headed off in her direction in the first place, sped toward home.

Suddenly there was a long shadow in the middle of his right headlight beam, and just as suddenly it was gone.

Pete swerved to the left, slammed on his brakes, and jumped out of the truck. He couldn't have hit someone, it hadn't felt like it, but still he raced around to the right side of the truck and looked at the ground. When he looked back up, there was Travis Dearborn, leaning against the hood.

Pete grabbed Travis by the shoulders and turned him toward the light. "Did I hit you?" Travis leaned his face away, but not before Pete could see that he had been crying.

"Are you all right?"

"I'm all right," said Travis.

"I didn't hit you?"

"No."

"What are you doing?" Pete became aware that his voice was excessively strident, and he lowered it to a more human range and tried again. "What are you doing on this road in the dark?"

Travis didn't answer at first. He looked away, behind him, toward the beach. "Practice."

"It's a bad road at night. Let me give you a lift."

Travis shook his head. He dashed a hand across his eyes and straightened up, no taller than Pete, but compared to Pete's hospital-weakened frame, he seemed infinitely more lithe and powerful as he moved onto the shoulder and began walking toward Shore Road.

"I'm going that way," Pete called after him, aware as he said it that it must sound a little strange since his truck was heading the *other* way.

"I'm okay." The sound of Travis's voice was muffled,

74

as if the night's fog had settled in front of him at just that moment, but he raised a hand and waved behind him, and Pete realized there was not really anything else he could do. He climbed back into his truck, and since he had said he was going that way, turned around and drove on until he reached Shore Road.

Why was Travis crying? Pete remembered the rocky scene he had witnessed between Carlisle and Travis at the Browns', thought about Travis refusing the job at Factotum and Henry accepting it, and wondered if perhaps the relationship between Carlisle and Travis was nearing an end. For some reason he hoped not, but he could think of no other reason for Travis to be crying. Had he failed to live up to some expectation, some new demand that the grieving Carlisle had thrust upon him? It didn't seem fair for her, even in her sorrow, to expect from Travis behavior he had no idea how to provide.

With a slam and a jolt, Pete's thoughts returned to Connie, and he felt again a small twinge of that anger he had felt when he had last sat with her in this truck. He had demanded some explanations then, some answers for her abrupt departure with Glen Newcomb, and for her suddenly coming back, alone. He had gotten no answers, but he knew that in some inexplicable way he had enjoyed the anger, and he felt himself riding on that wave of remembered anger all the way around Shore Road onto Pease Street and up to the Coolidges' garage.

Her light was on, and there was her Triumph out front, that ridiculous midlife-crisis car she had come home to the island in. She had always wanted Pete to get rid of his old truck, never understanding how attached he was to it, how attached he was to his little cottage, to Factotum, to Nashtoba and the people who lived there. Without allowing himself further thought, Pete parked the truck behind the Triumph, got out, and banged on the door on the side of the garage.

Pete heard rapid, muffled footsteps coming from somewhere above, and he pictured her long, tan legs, her bare feet on the steps, her body graceful even as she fired herself down the stairs. What would she be wearing? In the old days it would have been one of his own flannel shirts, but whose shirts would she be wearing now?

Before the footsteps inside had quite reached the bottom, he turned and fled.

"Motive," said Willy McOwat, into his beer. They were not, this time, at Lupo's, but sitting at Willy's kitchen table in the small, ugly ranch house he was renting until he decided if he and Nashtoba could learn to live with each other. The chief lived down a dirt road near the intersection of Pease Street and Shore Road, just where Pete had found himself shortly after fleeing Connie. The house was the house of someone who wasn't in it very much; there were no pictures on the walls, few dishes in the cupboards, and mostly beer in the fridge.

"I can't figure who'd want to kill Bentley, I can't figure there's anyone she could have stirred up enough to get that mad," continued the chief.

"I still think it was an accident," said Pete, concentrating hard on Bentley so as not to think of anything else, such as what an idiot he was.

Willy snorted. "You saw the back of her head? Some accident. About twenty blows. No, I figure there's only one reason for anybody to kill Bentley, and that has to do with the fact that she was knocked up."

Pete winced. "Her sister seems to think that something was troubling her. She said she wasn't herself, wasn't around much, wasn't—"

Willy slammed a huge hand down on the table. "And why didn't she tell *me* that?"

Pete, taken aback by this uncharacteristic outburst, decided to ignore it. "But her being pregnant could certainly explain all of that, don't you think?"

"Pregnant, and nobody knew about it. There had to be a reason for the big secret, a reason why she couldn't trust anyone, not even her sister, with the news, and the reason must be more important than the pregnancy itself, maybe involving someone who would be in more trouble than Bentley herself, somebody married, say. And the only thing that louses up that whole idea is this goddamned ring, the ring of some high school kid, some junior.''

"Henry's ring was stolen from his gym locker," Pete said.

Willy put down his beer and stared at Pete. "Henry's was stolen."

"At least that's what Carlisle says." Pete reiterated what he had been told about Henry's ring.

"He's sure it got stolen from his locker?"

"Don't ask me," said Pete. "For all I know, he never even ordered one; I'm just passing on what I'm told."

"He ordered one, all right," said Willy. "Only one guy never ordered one, someone named—" Willy began to pat his pockets, first the one in the blue cotton work shirt he was wearing, then he stood up and began banging at the ones in his jeans. Finally he retrieved a tiny, mangled notebook, out of which he read the name. "Sunderland. Martin. That's the guy who didn't order a ring."

Pete knew Marty Sunderland. Pete had tutored Marty the previous spring, in a last-ditch effort to prevent him from having to repeat his junior year, but Marty had had his mind on other things, and so Marty was still a junior. He worked at the supermarket after school and was supposed to be saving up for college, assuming he could pull his grades out of the gutter. Pete didn't imagine class rings were too high on Marty's list right now. But wait a minute. Marty stayed back . . .

"Marty stayed back," said Pete. "Marty would have had a class ring from *last* year."

"So what? You figure he still wears it? So what? The ring you found belonged to one of the juniors *this* year."

Yes. Of course. Marty's ring, whether he still wore it or not, didn't much matter, since the date on it was this year's.

"So in other words," Willy continued, "what you're telling me is that anyone could have killed Bentley, dropped his own ring, and stolen someone else's to cover up.''

"Or someone could have dropped his ring months ago," said Pete. "Totally unrelated."

"Thanks. This beach is a popular place? Seems kind of out of the way to me."

The point precisely, Pete wanted to say, but he didn't. No wonder this guy was still a bachelor. Actually, the beach beyond the marsh in front of Factotum wasn't all that out of the way, not as out of the way as some other places on the island, the caves, for instance—the cliffs on the other side of the woods by the school dropped off into caves that riddled the earth with tunnels and pockets, some of which had broken through from above to leave treacherous, overgrown pitfalls into the earth. The caves were difficult to get to by land or sea, making them just about perfect, for some things.

"Sometimes the kids who live down-island cut along my road and up the beach from school. I nearly killed Travis Dearborn there tonight, as a matter of fact." Pete said no more about that encounter. Travis's tears, Pete decided, were nobody's business but Travis's, and anyway, the chief didn't seem too interested.

Pete, on the other hand, couldn't help continuing to wonder if Carlisle and Travis had indeed broken up. He felt peculiarly caught up with it, somehow bonded to Travis by his tears, somehow distrustful of Carlisle for causing them, and the only thing that seemed to supplant them in his mind as he lay exhausted yet awake in bed some hours later was when he finally grew tired enough to allow himself to think of Connie, and Glen, and what a fool he had been.

# Chapter
# 8

The phone rang beside Connie's bed and she nearly jumped out of her skin. She had been jumpy for hours, ever since she had run downstairs to find no one at her door and had seen what for a minute she had foolishly thought were Pete's taillights disappearing around the bend.

"What!" she hollered into the phone.

"It's Willy McOwat." His voice was calm and controlled in comparison to her own, and she narrowed her eyes with suspicion and looked at the clock. It was eleven-fifteen. And what was this *Willy McOwat* stuff? Wasn't he supposed to identify himself as the chief? Weren't we getting a little informal here?

"What," Connie repeated, but despite herself, it came out merely cranky instead of angry. She was tired, and it required a certain amount of energy to maintain a head of steam.

"I'm sorry to bother you so late, but I did need a piece of important information. There are other ways to get it, as I'm sure you must know, but I have my reasons for preferring to find out this way if I can. I wondered if you were able to observe the juniors and to determine if anyone was missing a class ring. I can tell you that everyone but Martin Sunderland should be in possession of one, and I know from other sources that Henry Tourville claims that his was stolen—"

"Stolen!" Connie slid her bare feet out of bed, felt the chilled floor, and curled them up underneath her instead. Stolen. She felt an odd relief. She attempted to ignore what the use of the word "claims" implied.

"From his gym locker, apparently. Or so Pete tells me."

*Pete???* How the hell did *Pete* get into this? And what was with the sudden meaty silence on the other end of the line?

"I wanted to check out a few things with you before I spoke with Henry. I believe it was his essay that involved the wife and the lover and the blowtorch?"

Connie stared at the phone receiver in disbelief. It wasn't possible that this idiot was going to implicate Henry Tourville on the basis of an essay he wrote for her class and a stolen ring. "I fail to see . . ." she began, and then stopped. The more she stalled, the worse she would make it for Henry. "Yes, it was his," she finished, in what she was proud to note was a perfectly controlled tone of voice.

"Hey," said the chief. "Don't start blaming me for all this. I'm sure you can see that if there's anyone else missing a ring, I should know about it. I'm trying to keep out of the school, since those kids spook—or should I say, solidify?—pretty easily."

Again, silence. Connie had the feeling that if she never spoke again, the silence wouldn't rattle this man in the least. And why the hell *should* she speak? Why should she blow the whistle on Alan Anderson?

"Not that the rings are really all that significant. In fact, if it turns out that Henry's locker really was broken into, the ring means very little, if anything at all. Still, for the purpose of neatness, if you had anything helpful to add, I'd like to hear it. Pete seems to favor the accident theory himself."

Connie snorted. "He would! He thinks that nothing bad can ever happen as long as you brush your teeth every

night!'' And suddenly a strange kind of wistfulness over-
whelmed her.

More silence, and oddly enough, when the chief spoke
again, he sounded half-wistful himself. *"Was* there anyone
else without a ring that you noticed?''

"What makes you so sure I'd notice at all? It's not as
if—''

He cut her off again. "I think you'd notice. I'm sure you
did notice. I think you'd have more trouble ignoring than
noticing the ring situation after what I passed on to you the
other night. Of course, if you still feel like a rat . . .''

With tremendous effort, and several deep breaths, Connie refrained from saying quite a few things that it suddenly
occurred to her to say. Immediately following that brief but
intense struggle she was filled with a sense of futility and
an extreme exhaustion. Suddenly she wanted very badly to
go to sleep, and she knew it didn't much matter what she
said to get this pain in the ass off the phone. "Alan Anderson has no ring,'' she said. "Now may I go to sleep?''

"Almost,'' said the chief, sounding all at once rather
down. "Just one more question. The gym teacher is Roy
Millis? There's no one else in charge of the men's locker
room?''

"I am not intimate with the workings of the men's locker
room.''

"Thank you. I'm sorry to have bothered you. Good
night.''

"Good night,'' said Connie, much more pleasantly than
she would have thought possible.

"Good night,'' he said again, sounding really very sad,
almost. Connie hung up the phone, looked at it for a few
seconds, got into bed, closed her eyes, and lay there, wide-
awake.

The door to the classroom slammed behind her, and Connie nearly jumped through the roof. "Alan!'' she hollered.

"What!'' he hollered back, and Connie closed her eyes
briefly in an attempt to regain control of herself. Nothing

Pete had ever cooked up for them at Factotum had been this hard!

"You're late," said Connie, her calm restored by sheer force of will, "and please don't slam the door."

"It's not my fault and I've got a note, ma'am," said Alan, setting off a few giggles. "Spent half the stupid morning trying to tell the cops when I lost my ring."

Connie turned around and stared at him as he wound his way down the aisle toward the back. Mumbling and hissing sounds issued in his wake, but not the startling-new-evidence-in-the-courtroom kinds of sounds. Nobody seemed exactly bowled over by the news, least of all Alan. When he got opposite Travis Dearborn, he fake strangled him. "And if you don't give it back, I'll kill you, I swear it!" The class laughed. Most of them. Connie noticed that Henry Tourville's eyes had narrowed and that Carlisle Brown was staring at Alan. Alan strangled a few more of his classmates, girls this time, and the crowd whooped it up in appreciation. Almost everyone, male or female, got a kick out of Alan, but Connie had a feeling that he still didn't have the kind of draw that Travis did. Connie fully suspected that whatever, or whoever, Travis wanted, Travis got.

Travis had chosen as his seat that morning not his usual one next to Carlisle, but one farther in the back of the room, well within the range of Natalie Price's web. Even before Alan had arrived, there seemed to be a certain current in the air, and Connie wondered if all this meant that Travis had bounced Carlisle. All the girls had seemed extra perky, at any rate, and Connie tried not to think about Travis dumping Carlisle a week after her sister was found dead on the beach. Didn't decency count for anything anymore? And what *was* going on in this room? Why did everyone look as if a missing ring was old news? Why did no one seem to think there was anything odd about it? What did they *know?* Something.

"When did you say you missed your ring, Alan?"

"Dunno, for sure."

"My ring appears to be missing also," said Henry. "And as it happens, I do know just when that occurred. It was stolen out of my gym locker last Wednesday afternoon."

"You should tell the police, Henry," Connie said. "Tell them that your ring was stolen." It was the best she could do, knowing they already knew, knowing that for some reason she wanted Henry to appear to have nothing to hide in the chief's eyes.

"They spoke to me also, this A.M. I believe it must have been shortly before they stopped in on Alan. I explained my situation, they had checked my locker, but I believe it had been sufficiently vandalized in the past as to be inconclusive about this present incident."

"Oh," said Connie. No one else said anything at all. As Connie looked around the room, eight pairs of eyes were suddenly and instantly absorbed with things in their own notebooks or on their desks.

As Connie lugged her books down the nearly empty corridors at the end of the day, she found herself looking down at the institutional beige and tan linoleum floors. What was she looking for, class rings? Alan's was lost. Henry's was stolen. That meant that the ring on the beach could belong to anyone. But someone was going to have to convince the chief that Henry's ring *was* stolen. On Wednesday. In the boy's locker room, where Roy Millis reigned. It just figured it would have to be Roy Millis. Connie didn't imagine Roy would say anything to her that he wouldn't say to the chief, and it was hardly worth putting up with him for an entire evening, but she still had to speak to him to worm her way out of their date somehow, and maybe while she was speaking to him, she could find out a thing or two. Connie decided to leave the building by way of the gym to see if he was still there, knowing that he was most likely long gone, knowing he was not the type to linger after the bell, knowing he was . . . sitting at his desk in the phys ed office with his feet up, picking at his teeth with an index card.

Before Connie could reconsider, he was up and out of the room, walking beside her with a hand on her shoulder.

"Oh, I knew today was the big day the minute I woke up, and I've thought of nothing else since! Now, where shall we go? What shall we do?"

Connie glared at him. "We'll get into all that in a minute, but first I want to know something. Henry Tourville's ring got stolen out of his gym locker a week ago Wednesday, Roy. Know anything about it?"

Roy Millis stopped dead in his tracks and slammed his hand against his heart. "You couldn't be *accusing* me? Me, Roy Millis? Roy I. Millis, middle initial I for Integrity? Although I must confess to you I have always possessed a burning desire to own a Nashtoba High School ring. Imagine the glory, the prestige, the—"

"Oh, cut the crap, Roy. I just want to know if Henry told you about it, or if you saw it, or if you noticed his locker having been jimmied, or anyone hanging around it, or—"

"Assuming, firstly, that I know which locker is Henry's. Assuming I know which cherub is Henry. Assuming I was in the locker room as was my duty, instead of lingering outside your door, mooning at you through the—"

Connie opened her mouth to say something really foul-mouthed and happened just then to catch sight of Maxine Peck, outside the doors to the gym, peering through one of the small squares of glass.

"Maxine!"

Maxine jumped nearly as well as Connie had been doing of late.

"Whew! Hi." She looked at Roy Millis, then looked away. She seemed pale and tired.

"Listen, Roy," said Connie. "About tonight. I can't do it. I . . ."

Roy Millis studied her keenly, and for once said nothing.

"When you said Tuesday, I wasn't thinking Tuesday, I was thinking Wednesday. I wasn't thinking at all, actually. I can't do it. I—"

"Wednesday will also be fine," said Roy, still watching her, and Connie, for once in her life, found herself disconcerted enough to have nothing to say. It was her own stupid fault that she was in this mess, she knew, and she also knew that it was going to be an extremely ugly night. But what if he did have something to say to her about Henry's ring? Standing here in the hall was certainly not the place to get into it, and maybe later he would feel more free to discuss the students and the ring and the dead Bentley and . . . Connie brought herself up short, amazed at how all of a sudden the idea of talking to Roy Millis was almost beginning to sound appealing. Was she *that* lonely? Was she that desperate for a friendly ear? She looked Roy straight in the eye and answered, "Wednesday," nothing more, and Roy gave his ridiculous little half bow. Connie joined Maxine at the gym door and, peering through the glass door on her side, was not surprised to see Travis Dearborn doing what was probably his two-thousandth push-up on the other side. She looked at Maxine again; as she saw her white face turn to fuchsia, Connie made a humphing sound to herself. She was getting pretty damned sick of Travis, for no reason that was anywhere close to being his fault, but there it was.

"Wednesday," Roy reiterated unnecessarily from behind her. "I'll pick you up at eight! Don't be late!"

Maxine pulled her gaze away from the sight of Travis's gleaming bare flesh just long enough to give Connie an extremely disgusted look.

Connie jerked a thumb at Roy, who didn't seem to have enough sense to be grateful that it wasn't a finger, but finally he took the cue and left.

"Miss your bus?" Connie asked Maxine. "Want a ride?"

Maxine looked through the glass again and sighed, apparently weighing the chances of Travis Dearborn cutting the rest of practice and walking her home, or even saying boo to her if she waited around until he finished. Reality seemed to glimmer. "Okay," she said.

It had never occurred to Connie that she wouldn't be driving Maxine home to her own house.

"Here!" Maxine yelled, as Connie was about to sail past

the road to Factotum, and Connie twirled the little car around the corner without understanding right away.

Here?? Factotum? The road to Factotum was narrow, tar-on-the-bottom-and-sand-and-gravel-on-the-top, and un-named. Connie's old address when she had lived there had officially read, "Off Shore Road, Nashtoba," but things addressed simply "Nashtoba" always got there just as fast. She tried to tell herself that those days gone by, over a whole year gone by, had nothing to do with her anymore, that she was driving Maxine to Factotum to meet her mother and that that was all that Factotum meant to her now. Still, as she rounded the last hill of spiky beach plum bushes and saw the winking windows below the sharply angled roof, all she could think of was one word: home.

Connie's eyes began to sting with tears, and she became furious with herself. Pete's truck was there, of all the damned luck, and if he ever saw her pull up to Factotum *crying,* for God's sake . . . She tried to remember why she had left. She couldn't.

The front door to Factotum opened and Pete came out. He started toward his truck, then saw her car and stopped dead in his tracks, raising a hand to shade his eyes as if he couldn't quite believe what he was seeing. Looking at him standing there in what Connie could have sworn were the same old jeans and the same green flannel shirt they had cut off him in the hospital, she couldn't remember anything except that he had been nearly knifed to death by some lunatic, and any minute she was going to really get bawling.

"Out," she said to Maxine.

"Don't you—"

"Out!"

Maxine got out.

Connie fled.

# Chapter
# 9

Pete stood on the lawn long after Maxine had gone inside, unable to recall just where it was he had been planning to go in such a hurry not minutes before. *That stupid car,* he was thinking in one part of his brain, while another part was registering the look of the scene in an entirely other light: Connie's hair still streaky-gold from summer, a mishmash of uncaptured long ends flying every which way against the dark green of the car, sea green eyes flashing. Out of the confusion inside his head Pete finally sorted one truth—Connie didn't want to see him. So that was that. But he continued to stand on the lawn like a fool, looking down the road, until a raised voice from inside the cottage snapped him back to the situation at hand.

"What do you want out of me?" It was Carlisle, whom Pete had last seen in the back room sorting out newspapers. It was loud. Too loud. Pete jogged up to the door, hopped the step, and raised his eyebrows in answer to Rita's expression as he headed for the hall.

"I'm sick of you pestering me! I'm not going to the Shack, I'm not going to the game, I'm not going anywhere. And I'm not going with you! Would I be coming here every day after school if I wanted to see people? Would I be hiding in this room if I wanted to see *you?*"

Maxine's back was to Pete, but Carlisle's face, visible

over Maxine's shoulder, was white with angry red splotches. Maxine didn't remain facing her long—she turned, shoved at Pete in the doorway, and bolted out of the room—and Pete, who found himself suddenly weighing the advantages of wintering in Florida, was left facing Carlisle alone.

"Well," he began.

"I'm sorry. I mean I'm *sorry,* but she's driving me *nuts!*" She stepped haltingly toward Pete, waiting for him to move out of the way, but the minute Pete opened his mouth, she started screaming. "Don't! Don't *say* anything! Just move, will you please?"

He moved. Carlisle ran out of Factotum, and Pete walked back and sat down on his corner of Rita's desk. Maxine was nowhere in sight.

"Carlisle's not herself," said Rita.

"No," said Pete.

"Maxine tore off for the beach."

"Oh." He looked toward the still open door. "Where's Henry?"

"Painting Meecham's shutters. Carlisle wanted to stay here and sort papers, so I let her. She seemed like she wanted to be alone."

Pete was beginning to see her point.

Talk of Meecham's shutters had reminded him that he had been going to Beston's to buy some wood glue. "Maybe I'll pop down to the beach for a minute," he said instead. Rita laid a cold hand over his. Her hands were always cold when she was worried. He turned his over and gave hers a quick squeeze, then popped off the desk to go look for Maxine.

"She's not herself," Pete found himself repeating, some minutes later, to the profile of the girl who sat on the sand, her arms wrapped around her knees.

"You're telling *me!* Like I even care if she goes to the old Shack with me or not! I tell you, she is *weird!* I come up behind her and she jumps ten feet in the air and starts *screaming* at me! I see her coming up the beach and I say to her later, what were you doing at the beach, and she says she wasn't *at* the beach! She's losing her *mind!* It's like . . ." Maxine frowned at the ebbing tide, her gaze, Pete was sure, locked on the rocks where Bentley's body had been trapped. Suddenly she jumped up, all the color running out of her face and then flooding back. "If I tell you something . . ." she began, but whatever had possessed her to begin seemed to hinder her from finishing.

"Anything you want to tell me goes no further, Max, you know that."

"Not even to the police?"

Pete frowned. He was staring to feel glad that he wasn't a father. But Maxine wasn't stupid; he had a feeling that if he just redefined things for her a bit . . . "You're saying you want me to keep something secret that the police ought to know, is that what you're saying?"

"Yes," said Maxine. "Or I mean maybe. I'm not sure, and I don't want them to know unless I'm sure. I just wanted to see what you thought about it, that's all."

Pete looked up at her, at the jumble in her brown eyes and the pinched look on her face, and his heart went out to her. Once he had thought that it was enough to be her friend; now he knew otherwise. She already had friends, and father or no, he felt a certain responsibility here. "Let's put it this way, Maxine. If I hear you out and feel that the police should be told, I'll tell you that, and leave it up to you to tell them. I'll trust you to tell them."

"And if I don't, you will, is that it?"

Pete squinted at her. "Maybe I will and maybe I won't," he replied. "I'm not going to promise you more than that when I don't know what I'm promising."

*"Great,"* said Maxine, in just exactly the way her mother was known to say "fine," and things were just as clearly not great when she said it as they were not fine when her mother did.

They walked back to Factotum in silence, Pete futilely wracking his brain the whole way for something he could or should add that would allow her to speak and yet give him room to maneuver, should it be something about which he absolutely could not remain silent.

Afterward, when Pete had spent many hours trying to make sense of many things, it occurred to him that it could have been that scene on the beach with Maxine that set him off. It could also have been Maxine's fight with Carlisle. In actual fact, though, it was Ree.

Jimmy Solene was again in the yard, leaning on his rake, when Pete pulled in for his promised meal at the Browns'. His truck was the only vehicle in sight, so Pete assumed that Carlisle had already gone wherever it was she had been going, and had gone in Ree's jeep. He parked his truck well clear of Jimmy's and knocked on the door.

No answer. He knocked again, louder, and from somewhere up above his head he heard a window open. "Pete? Up here!" Ree sang out, and Pete pushed open the door and looked up the stairs.

"Here," the voice called again.

Pete moved up the stairwell following the sound. Through an open door on his right, he saw her sitting on the edge of a bed that must once have belonged to Bentley. The room was full of dormered west light, the walls and furniture were freshly painted white, and the curtains and quilted covering on the bed were pink and white roses. The end table near the bed and the top of the dresser were covered with lacy white cloths, and still laid out neatly were Bentley's comb and brush and some assorted boxes and bottles. In contrast to the perfectly appointed room, Ree was wearing old pea green corduroys that had worn pale at the knees and a rust-colored sweater that was stretched and faded. Around her on the bed lay a pile of clothes, and an array of half-full cardboard boxes was scattered around her feet.

Ree looked up at him and smiled, her face a map of fatigue, strain, and tears. She picked up a pink sweater, then let it drop. "Brand-new. I think in the last three months that girl must have spent two years of savings on clothes." She looked around her. "And on this room."

Pete walked into the room, brushing Ree's shoulder with his fingers in lieu of coming up with anything more comforting. "Do you have to do this now? Maybe you should give it some time, let someone help you."

Ree shook her head, wiped her eyes, didn't move. "I want to do it. I want to finish it. But I didn't mean to be doing it right now, I lost track of how late it was and I—"

The front door slammed and Ree jumped into the end table, the glass base of the lamp rattling Bentley's white alarm clock.

"Ma!"

Ree looked up at Pete and didn't speak. If Pete didn't know better, he would have sworn she looked afraid. "Coming!" she called, and pushed herself up off the bed, heading past Pete toward the door. She hadn't made it that far before the pounding feet had reached the hall and Carlisle began talking, an anger that seemed out of proportion to the subject matter underlining her words.

"I can't believe that creep Jimmy Solene hasn't finished this yard yet," she said. "I mean how long can it take to rake four—" She rounded the doorway and stopped in her tracks.

Carlisle was, Pete noticed, wearing the same clothes she had had on that afternoon at Factotum—a pair of ripped jeans and a purple sweatshirt that had "Boo" slashed across the front in big black letters, and "Hiss" across the back. Her hair was springing every which way, her eyes full of the same anger Pete had seen earlier that afternoon. Her face was rapidly turning salmon pink as she looked first around the room and then at her mother. *"What are you doing?"*

Ree backed up from the doorway where Carlisle stood. "It has to be done, Carlisle."

*"Keep out of here. Keep out of my stuff."*

"These are Bentley's things, Carlisle. You can't keep

everything, there isn't room, and you didn't like her new things anyway."

Carlisle moved over to the nearest carton and began to unload it, throwing things onto the bed behind her mother. "I'll tell you what I don't like, but until I do, I don't want you touching this room!" She ran over to the bureau and yanked open the smallest drawer on the left. Her eyes darted back and forth over its contents, and seeming to see everything she had hoped to see right where she hoped to see it, she exhaled audibly and turned around to face them, pressing her back against the drawers. "Get out of here."

"Carlisle!" Ree's voice was sharp and hard, and suddenly Pete wanted very much to go home. He had gotten fairly adept at defusing Maxine and Rita, but this was a whole different kettle of feelings, and he was in no position to try to be of use. Besides, as he looked from one Brown to the other, Pete got the distinct impression that neither of these two really needed his help. As he began to edge out of the room, their angry voices exploded behind him.

"Will you think what you're saying?" That was Ree.

"Will *you* think what you're doing!" That was Carlisle.

"I have a guest. I have no time to talk about this now." That was Ree again, and Pete, the guest, moved further off, passing Carlisle's room, which was easily distinguishable by the clash of posters all over walls and ceiling. He hit the stairs, his sneakers soft on the treads, but apparently not soft enough.

"You *had* a guest," said Carlisle, and Ree hurried out of the room. The door to Bentley's room closed loudly, though not exactly with a slam, and Pete was sure that Carlisle was going to stay in there until she had it put back to rights.

"I'm so sorry," said Ree. "We never fight, you may not believe that, but none of us, we never did, at least not until recently. I just don't know what's been happening. First Bentley going off into these black moods, and now Carlisle . . . I don't know what's got into her."

It seemed pretty obvious to Pete.

"I mean imagine, dredging up all this animosity toward Jimmy Solene!"

Pete *could* imagine it, but why, considering everything that had just gone on, Ree seemed to want to talk about Jimmy Solene, he *couldn't* imagine.

"I mean really," Ree went on. "I only hired him because he came around one day, and it isn't that he doesn't do the work."

Pete didn't much care what Jimmy did or didn't do, and was still secretly trying to figure a way to go home, but Ree led him into the living room and sat him down on the couch, plopping down beside him with an exhausted sigh. Neither of them spoke.

When Carlisle came back downstairs, Pete was somehow not surprised to see that she had changed into a conservative tan skirt and the pink sweater that Ree had picked up a moment before.

"I'm sorry," she said to her mother, and then she turned to Pete and swallowed. "Will you tell Maxine I'm sorry also?"

"Sure," said Pete. "Don't worry about it."

Pete watched her until she was out the door.

"That was Bentley's sweater?"

"No," said Ree. "It wasn't." She looked white and shaken.

"Ree," Pete began, about to offer to postpone their evening to a time when she was more up for company, but before he could say anything else, she turned toward him and brushed his mouth with her lips, a preliminary, fleeting touch that she repeated until he responded, until they had turned it into something longer, something . . . slower. Pete's hands slid around her as if on some hunt of their own, but even as they did so, some niggling little part of him *still* felt like he wanted to go home. He supposed that should have told him something. He supposed it should have told him a whole lot.

Much, much later Pete looked down his own scrawny, sweaty length to the rumpled red head resting on his belly and tried to ignore the searing sensation under his ribs and the nagging unease at the back of his brain. His gaze traveled over Ree's relaxed, sun-bronzed body, and for some reason he found himself reminded of what Carlisle had said about her mother. Her mother the prude. He looked at Ree again. What was wrong with this picture? And what was he doing in it? She had practically dragged him up the stairs, shoved a condom into his hand and grabbed at his shirt . . .

Was it possible that Ree was, well . . . *after* him? No. Something did not compute. He could still see it as if he had filmed it, every second of the first time he and Connie had gone to bed together, how after knowing each other all those months, one certain look between them had suddenly carried them out of their clothes . . .

Pete lifted Ree and shifted her body, placing her head gently down on the pillow beside him. Her eyes fluttered open, she smiled, then her eyes closed again. Pete pulled the sheet over her and began to look around for his clothes.

Pete swung by Willy's house, but the Scout wasn't there, and Pete was surprised at the sharpness of his disappointment, surprised to find how much he had been counting on talking to his friend. He swung along Shore Road, not thinking about anything until he found himself driving past Mable's and the freshly painted sign swinging in the dark.

But Connie didn't want to see him.

All the same, he should, sometime, thank her.

And he didn't have to stay long after all.

For a minute he was sure that it was his old, washed-out blue work shirt she was wearing, and then a second later, as she realized who he was and had grabbed at the top of her head in that crazy way she always did when she was surprised and didn't know what to do with her arms, he thought, no, of course it isn't my shirt.

Connie dropped her arm, her hair now mussed and looking as if she had just gotten up, and the pain of the memory was almost enough to pull him straight out the door and back home. Was that why he had come here tonight? Had he needed to see her to test himself, to test what he had doubted he had had with Ree? Connie was looking right at him, right into him, also trying to figure out, Pete knew, what he was doing there, and his glance skated over her eyes and down the straight nose to her mouth, and he wished she were at least smiling.

"You look like hell," she said.

*She* looked terrific. Connie had always been long and lean and angular, but now there was more flesh on the bare bone and muscle, and he couldn't stop staring at the change in her, half-afraid to look away in case he missed something else. He knew he should go now before he started dwelling on her further, but Connie was already turning. In slow motion, with crablike side steps, she was moving up the stairs, and Pete, unable to look away from her eyes, her sea green eyes, followed her up and up.

"You look . . . heavier," he said, once they had reached the top of the stairs and were standing side by side.

"I *am* heavier," she answered, and she grinned, not what just anyone would do after hearing something like that, and Pete interpreted it to mean that she knew how good she looked, knew how, by not doing anything but standing there in bare feet and baggy pants and someone else's shirt, she could force him to remember every inch of what was underneath . . . He had no business being here. He turned around.

"Hey! You came to tell me I'm fat? That's it?" Her hand clutched his elbow fast, dropping it even faster.

"I came to say thank you," said Pete, the words sounding to his own ears like something his mother was making him say. "For helping out this summer." And then, just in case she might be thinking that he was thinking that she had done it for him, for some particular reason, he added, "Rita was very grateful. It meant a lot to her."

He watched the green eyes cloud over, lose interest. Was she wishing he would leave?

"How is Rita?"

"Fine," said Pete.

"Maxine?"

"Oh, all right, I guess."

"Well, if Maxine is only all right, then Rita's not fine at all," said Connie, and Pete felt a peculiar and unreasonable anger rising. What did she know about it anymore?

"But I'll tell you one thing that could be troubling Maxine—Travis Dearborn. I think she's in love."

"Oh," said Pete. Was that what she had wanted to talk to him about on the beach? Travis Dearborn?

"And you've got Carlisle back now, I hear," Connie went on. "So I guess things could get interesting over there. Carlisle seems to be doing better. I've been kind of worried about her, she's been pretty down. Of course, it's done wonders for her schoolwork. She just handed in her first paper in three years that was on time, or so I seem to see from her past record. Of course, I don't think the course of true love is running too smooth—"

Abruptly Connie stopped talking.

"Yeah," Pete said, "true love'll do it every time," and listened in dismay as what he had intended to be light banter came out like a decree from the pope.

For just about the first time since he'd known her, Connie's eyes avoided direct contact with his, and Pete felt something hard and piercing inside of him that had nothing to do with scar tissue pressing on nerves.

"So! You want a beer?"

Pete hesitated, frozen, and was not surprised when she seemed to read his thoughts.

"For chrissake! I said a beer. Stop analyzing every possible ramification of sitting down with me for a drink and just do it, will you?"

Pete sat.

Connie rattled on, and Pete looked around him as she talked, at the picture he had given her, the only picture on the walls, at the tiny dimensions of the world she now lived in, tinier even than the home he had once shared with her on the marsh, and waves of guilt smashed into him. But wait a minute. This wasn't *his* fault, this was *her* fault; *she* was the one who left! From that faultily capped well within him he felt his fury begin to rise.

"I confess I'm a little worried about Henry," Connie said, and Pete resurfaced into the present.

"I mean I know the chief is thinking about him a lot these days. First there's the ring, and then there's the essay, and then there's—"

"Essay?"

Connie explained about the essay. She also told him about Carlisle's blank page, the difficult time Carlisle had been having of late, her suspicions that Travis was not being very understanding about her grief, her relief that into the sudden void, along had come Henry.

Of *course*. Of course it would all be Travis's fault. Of course that snake-in-the-grass Henry would be standing there waiting for the breach, just so he could jump in and widen it. And of course it would be "poor Carlisle," Carlisle, who was running around flaunting Glen right under his very nose!

"Henry is being quite solicitous," Connie continued, and something inside Pete snapped.

"Which might also make sense if he'd just killed her sister," said Pete. "Feeling guilty, trying to make it up?"

Connie looked at him. "Henry Tourville did not kill her sister."

"Oh," said Pete. "End of discussion."

Connie put her beer down on the lobster trap with care. "All I'm saying is I've gotten to know them, that's all I'm saying. I think I can—"

"A whole month now, is it?"

Connie snatched up her beer but didn't drink it, her back ramrod-straight in the rocker. "I worked with the twins all summer, if you recall."

"We were talking about Henry, I thought. And I'm working with Henry now."

"And so am I! And I think I know Carlisle well enough

to know that she would never waste time on Henry Tourville unless he had one hell of a lot of integrity to offer, and that does not include murdering her sister. Henry Tourville is a courteous, polite—"

"Courteous! Polite!" scoffed Pete, and as he did so, he wondered at the peculiar comfort he was getting from all this. "Henry isn't Carlisle's type; Ree told me so. And she told me something else, too," Pete continued, only this very minute remembering Ree's remark about the Coke-bottle glasses. "It appears that old Henry was *Bentley's* type. How about that? How about if he got her pregnant and didn't want to face the consequences and bumped her off? How about that? And something else I picked up in one of my conversations with Ree—"

"Ree," said Connie. She reached across the lobster trap, picked up Pete's beer, which he was dismayed to find was already empty, and went into the little kitchenette to get two more from the refrigerator.

"Yes, Ree," Pete went on. "And I think Ree is intelligent enough and intuitive enough to be able to sort out who her daughters might like and who they wouldn't." All of a sudden Pete saw before him Glen Newcomb's own Coke-bottle glasses and was goaded on further, even as a secondary voice from somewhere between his brain and his spleen began asking him what the hell he thought he was doing. "And just because you seem to have become enamored of Henry doesn't necessarily mean that everyone else feels the same, now does it?"

Connie's head was still in the refrigerator when there was a knock at the door. She turned for the stairs without looking at him; when she came back, she had Willy McOwat with her. He was carrying a bottle of wine.

Wine.

At once Pete's face flushed hot and then drained cold. How dare they do this in front of him! He didn't stop to think that of the two visitors present, he was probably the only uninvited one, didn't feel any better at the thought that Willy didn't know Connie well enough not to bring her wine since she never drank anything but beer.

"Hey, Pete!" said Willy, clearly surprised to see him there. Pete nodded at him, but minimally.

"I have to go," he said.

"Hey, no," said Willy. "Don't let me interrupt anything. I can come back some other time. Really." He turned back toward the steps. "Enjoy your evening." He looked at Connie. Connie looked at Pete. Pete looked at the wine. Pouilly-Fuisse.

"No, really," he said, "I have to go. You enjoy *your* evening," and he thrust past Willy and down the stairs.

# Chapter 10

Connie glowered at the head of the stairs, resisting with supreme effort from removing the wine bottle from Willy's hands and chucking it at the back of Peter Bartholomew's head. Enjoy *your* evening! Connie whirled around and faced off in front of the police chief. "What the hell do you want now?"

The chief's eyes widened in what Connie interpreted to be mock surprise. "Want? I don't want anything. I came to thank you for your help. Here." He shoved the bottle at her, and if Connie had taken it from him, he probably would have exercised some decidedly superior judgment and followed Pete out the door, but Connie was immobilized by emotions that were running the gamut from despair to rage. She stared at the now empty stairwell until finally the chief moved into the kitchenette and put the bottle down on the counter.

"It was not my intention to interrupt anything," he ventured. "It had occurred to me that you were one of the few people around here who had been at all helpful, and I wanted to make sure you didn't think it went unnoticed."

"I'm sorry. I didn't mean to yell at you."

"Sure you did."

She sighed. She felt suddenly tired. "Yeah, I did. But

since you're here, you could tell me what the hell is going on. You're after Henry, aren't you?"

The chief shrugged and remained silent, watching her.

"Look," said Connie. "I don't give a damn what Ree Brown has been feeding Pete. Don't you have some scientific evidence that you resort to in times like this before you jump to the conclusion that it was Henry's baby?"

The chief looked toward the rocking chair and the lobster trap, but Connie refused to take him up on the hint. She crossed her arms and continued to stand there until he spoke.

"Henry's baby? The reason being that—"

"No reason at all as far as I can see. Bentley's mother telling Pete he was her type! I mean really! I should think it would take a little more than that before you charge off and assume things. Don't you do all that on the basis of blood tests now?"

"We can," said the chief, "but the same would apply there, as well. We can't just go around demanding blood out of everyone without something halfway reasonable in the way of suspicion."

Connie turned around, walked over to the rocking chair, and sat down. She breathed in and out twice, trying to calm herself down. Reasonable. Be reasonable. They were all going to be reasonable, and nothing was going to go astray just because Peter Bartholomew was off his rocker. And it was nice of the chief to bring the bottle, even if he did interrupt—

And of course, thought Connie, that was the whole crux of the matter, wasn't it? He hadn't interrupted anything. Ree Brown. She had *smelled* her on him, and that was the only reason he had come here, to throw Ree in her face, to see how many times he could squeeze her name into one four-minute conversation, to . . .

With an effort, Connie returned her attention to the chief. As soon as she did so, he spoke, and she was a bit taken aback by the turn in the conversation.

"You like it here?"

Connie nodded.

"But you left."

Connie looked away.

"You figure you'll stick around awhile this time?"

"I don't know. I guess so. I . . . I thought I wanted to be someplace else, anyplace else, and then once I got there, this place . . . I don't know. It gets to you, I guess."

"People too, I suppose."

Connie looked at him, but saw only a deep and impenetrable squint. Still, she thought she knew what he was talking about, and Connie was not one to be obscure if she could help it. "I guess people give up on each other faster than they do on places," she said, and wondered as she said it why she was telling it to this particular person. Was there something else in his eye?

"Oh, I don't know."

"I do." She really wished he'd stop squinting at her. She got up, went into the kitchenette, and stood there staring down at her bottle of wine. She supposed she was expected to offer him some, but she couldn't seem to get herself to move or speak. She could hear, and feel, the presence of the chief behind her long before his large, rough, and somehow comforting hand encircled her upper arm.

"I think I'd better go."

Either she was really starting to lose it or that statement was being posed in the form of a question. She half turned. Could it be she was right? She considered for a second what it would be like to thrash out a few of her frustrations with Willy, and she thought of Ree and of what a complete and total idiot Pete had been that very night, and still, when she did lift her eyes to meet the chief's, she knew what she was going to say before she said it. "I think, for now, you'd better." She watched his massive back as he went down the stairs, and it did occur to her to wonder what exactly she was trying to prove. Or to whom.

# Chapter
# 11

Pete wasn't much used to feeling this furious, and it didn't help things that he was totally confused as to whom he should be furious with. Well, maybe after all he wasn't so completely confused—he knew for certain that he should be furious with himself for the sorry ass he had been with Connie, but that didn't for a minute mean he couldn't be, shouldn't continue to be, furious with *her*. And wasn't he entitled to be pretty steamed up about Willy, sneaking in behind his back and seeing his wife like that? Ex-wife. Okay. He swung his truck around into Knackie's parking lot, in the mood for more beer, but tonight even this, it seemed, was not going to be done in peace.

Knackie's was over on the harbor side of the island, on the off side of Shore Road from the water, a sure sign that it was a fishermen's place. Pete knew that the reason they hung out there was that they didn't care if Knackie didn't bother to put out tablecloths as long as he was a fast draw with the beer. Pete could have gone to Lupo's, a place that in truth was a little more his style, with red and white cotton tablecloths, big, roomy booths, and a gleaming although much-dented bar, but Lupo's was on the other side of the island back near the causeway, and Knackie's was here, and in the mood he was in, Pete didn't much care about tablecloths either. He cocked a hip over the nearest available bar stool and, without thinking, ordered a Ballantine Ale, Connie's brand. He nodded to the familiar faces at the bar, not taking them in, making his nod only half of one so as to indicate that he wished to be left alone. But he wasn't two sips into his ale before he saw Jimmy Solene lift his long, slick head and pin his beer-sodden eyes on Pete from the other end of the bar. Pete looked hard into his beer, but it didn't help any—out of the corner of his eye he could see Jimmy ease himself off his stool and head in his direction.

"Hey, Pete Bartholomew!"

"Hey, Jimmy Solene." Pete stayed facing front, hoping he'd slide on by, but Jimmy Solene banged him on the left shoulder, forcing him to turn.

"I said hey!"

"And I said hey back." Oh, he was in no mood for this! He turned again toward his longed-for beer.

"You've been hanging out over Browns', I see."

Pete shook his head.

"I said you've been hanging out over Browns' and I seen you. What're you doing over there, huh?"

Pete couldn't believe this. He ignored Jimmy. Solene banged him on the shoulder again and Pete whipped around and jumped up off the stool. "Listen, Jimmy old pal," he said, and every head in the bar turn toward them. Pete took Jimmy by both shoulders and edged him back a few inches so that he had room to move past. He did it very unaggressively, he thought, but out of his peripheral vision he saw Leon Price, the bartender, glide down to the end of the bar where the hatch was, and nearer at hand, Ernie Ball slid off his bar stool and began to amble over. "It's none of your business what I'm doing over there, now is it, Jimmy?" said Pete, very calmly, very coolly.

Jimmy Solene leaned in closer to Pete's ear. "So which one are you sticking it to, Pete?" He rocked back on his heels, puffy chins jutting out from a neck and shoulders that were thicker than when Pete last got this close. A huge well of satisfaction surged up into Pete's chest as he hauled back and slammed his doubled-up fist into Jimmy's face.

"Aaaah!" Pete buckled over, grabbing his fist, feeling like the one who just got hit and probably looking like it too; Leon lunged forward, grabbed Jimmy Solene, and hustled him out of the bar.

*"God,* that hurts!" Pete flexed his fingers, surprised to see that they moved at all, and tried to shrug off the restraining arm of Ernie Ball, who had charged in a second later than Leon but in the more logical direction. The hand was swelling rapidly, Jimmy Solene was roaring a series of threats from outside the bar, and Pete's sense of fulfillment was fading, leaving him with a full load of self-disgust.

He feebly attempted to explain. "I owed him that."

Ernie Ball chewed on a bar straw and gazed out the door. "So now he owes you, and I hope she was worth it."

Pete stared at him, suddenly aware by his own slow grasp of Ernie's meaning how little Ree Brown had figured in his end of this whole ridiculous altercation, but he left the bar mulling over the various possibilities surrounding Jimmy's actions. It was, of course, the only logical explanation—Jimmy had either been peering in windows or making a good guess, and he had his own claim on that particular territory, was that it? Of course that was it. Pete knew better than to think that any woman in whom he might be interested would be unattached and waiting for *him,* and he was so awash in self-pity that he forgot for a good ten minutes that he had been strangely uninterested in the woman in question until now. Until now? What was he talking about? Was he going to take advantage of a situation just for the purpose of showing Jimmy Solene that he wasn't someone he could scare off? Pete's head was such a jumble of confusion that he didn't think about Connie and Willy for almost the whole ride home.

Hardy Rogers loomed over Pete's hand the next morning and tweaked at his fingers, waiting for Pete to wince. "Idiot."

"I think I should have hit him in the hand," said Pete, and Hardy gave a couple of short snorts of laughter as he tapped, none too gently, on one of the long bones that ran down the back of Pete's hand. "You've mucked up this fellow, I'd guess. Metacarpal. Nothing to take you off over, though."

*Take you off.* Hardy was using the island expression for crossing the causeway with an injury so severe that the hospital in Bradford was required. *Take you off* was the island equivalent to the slow drum roll in the movies, or maybe even the playing of taps. After the knifing, they had thrown Pete in an ambulance and taken him off. He had almost never come back *on,* and he found the joke to be in very poor taste.

"Rotated, too; see how this finger is crossing over right here? We'll have to get an X ray, and if I'm right, you'll have to have it immobilized, flexed like this for a while."

That was the thing Pete liked best about Hardy; he explained things. The only trouble was, the one thing Pete really wanted explained wasn't. "For a while. What does that mean, for a while?"

"Three or four weeks. That's for the *hand.* Now, to fix up what's between the ears, that's another matter entirely. What are you, thirty-six going on twelve?"

"You'd be a lot more help if you told me you'd spent half last night stitching up Jimmy Solene's face."

"Haven't seen the man. Sorry."


Everyone knew about Pete's run-in with Jimmy Solene long before his caged hand appeared in view. As usual, Hardy had been right, and when they got through fixing Pete up, the hand had become a cumbersome white club that was hurting him smartly. When Pete returned to Factotum, Rita was just terminating her fourth call on the matter. "Here he is now," Rita was saying into the phone, and passed it across the desk into Pete's left hand.

"Pete!" It was Ree. "Are you all right?"

"I'm fine," said Pete.

"I was so worried when I heard. What on earth possessed Jimmy Solene to—"

"I popped him one," said Pete, slightly ashamed to be feeling so proud. "It was nothing, just stupid, I—"

"Well, your friend the police chief was here this morning, and I told him he should speak to Jimmy about this. I mean really! I'm beginning to think Carlisle is not entirely out of line when she—"

"It was my fault," said Pete, feeling curiouser and curiouser about Ree. Shouldn't she be furious with him right now for walking out on her last evening? And why should she be so concerned about him and so ready to cast Jimmy Solene to the wolves after Jimmy had been working for her all this time, putting aside for the minute what other services he might have been performing for her as well? Again, something was wrong with this picture, but it wasn't a picture Pete wanted to dwell on any longer. "Why was the chief there this morning?" he asked instead.

"Oh, all this business about Henry being the father of Bentley's baby. He was going to get Henry right out of school after he left here. I just don't know what to think anymore. Henry's been so good to Carlisle in situations where Travis just hasn't seemed able to cope . . ." Ree's voice trailed off, leaving them hanging there on the phone, and Pete didn't know what to say to fill the air. Henry the father of Bentley's baby? Had there, after all, been some truth to the wild and vicious fabrication he had tossed in Connie's face the night before? The night before. The night before seemed on one hand very long ago, and on the other hand not nearly long enough.

"About last night," he began, but to his surprise, Ree cut him off and began apologizing herself.

"I know, I know, I don't know what got into me, I haven't been sleeping well, I think I was overtired, I didn't wake up for hours. You must have been starving. Did you wait around long?" She didn't wait for him to answer. She laughed again, sounding miserable, and Pete felt like a heel.

"Would you like to go out?" he asked her; it sounded about as amateur as it had the first time he had asked it, in the eleventh grade. "I mean, I could take *you* to dinner or something."

Silence.

"Or if there is something else you'd rather do . . ."

Ree gave a wild cackle of laughter, and Pete winced. "Dinner sounds very nice," she said, and all of a sudden Pete thought of sitting at Lupo's or someplace equally as exposed to the Nashtoba news hounds as he struggled to make conversation, and he opted for a more relaxing counteroffer.

"Or I could make you dinner here."

"Even better!" said Ree, and Pete tried to think of reasons why *she* should think so. Once again he couldn't come up with anything that he found himself able to believe.

Pete sank down into the cordgrass, leaned back against a driftwood piling that had washed up over the small dune on the edge of the marsh, propped his head on his good hand, and rested his aching one on his knee. He picked a stalk of fleabane and smelled it for the thousandth time, never quite believing the dusty rose blooms could smell so much like mothballs and mold.

He had spent a useless day trying unsuccessfully to do his usual tasks with just one hand, finally heading for the beach in frustration to sit and think about the things that he could be doing but didn't want to do. He had to shop for dinner, for one thing, but he didn't feel like shopping for dinner, didn't feel like running into anyone and explaining, again, about his hand. He gazed out over the Sound and its uncharacteristically still and glassy surface, and when he spied an alien form ambling down the beach in his direction, he realized he didn't want to run into anyone here either. Whoever it was raised his head, dashed a hand across his eyes, and looked right at Pete without seeing him; there among the tall grass he was all but invisible, and Pete sighed with relief. He watched the form move along the water's edge, skimming stones, and something about its power and grace made Pete realize that it was

Travis Dearborn even before Travis had come close enough for proper identification. He skimmed stone after stone, watching them skate over the surface of the water not ten yards from where Bentley had been found. Suddenly he looked down the beach in the direction from which he had come, and Pete, following his gaze, saw someone else approaching. Maxine. She began to run, that odd, hopping gait she had used not long ago to chase a "balloon." Pete could hardly bear to watch her. She ran right up to Travis, stopping too close to him. He reached out an arm as if to hold her, but instead stopped her and held her away. He looked past her, and Pete, following his gaze, saw two more figures coming down the beach: the bouncing red head could only be Carlisle, and the tall, wandlike figure was Henry Tourville. Henry had rested one hand on Carlisle's shoulder as he talked, his head bending down to hers now and then as they walked along. Pete looked back at Travis and Maxine and began to wish that he had left when leaving had been possible. All of a sudden Travis saw the couple down the beach and pushed past Maxine, his stride lengthening toward them. Carlisle laid a hand on Henry's arm, and he checked his stride briefly but then brushed her off and pushed on. Before Pete had a chance to interpret looks or body language, Travis walked right up to Henry and punched him in the gut.

*I* should have gone for the gut, Pete thought, and then, immediately ashamed of himself, scrambled to his feet. What was this, catching? He tore over the sand toward them, but his presence was unnoticed and apparently unneeded—Carlisle had inserted herself between the two men and was struggling with Travis, screaming at him at the top of her lungs.

"I hate you! I hate you!"

Pete reached them disgustingly out of breath. He peeled Carlisle's fingers out of Travis's shirt and backed Travis off three paces.

Travis, Pete was amazed to find, was sobbing. "It's *him! Him!*"

"I believe," said Henry Tourville from behind Pete, his voice sounding as breathless as Pete's but for other reasons, "that what we're experiencing here is a small impulse control problem."

"I mean it, Travis!" Carlisle was still shrieking. "This is it! I don't ever want to see you again!"

Travis didn't seem to have heard her. Pete, with his good hand still on Travis's chest, could feel Travis's body wracked with the gulping spasms of someone trying desperately not to cry. Pete almost felt like doing his crying for him.

"Come on," said Carlisle. She turned Henry around and headed them back in the direction from which they had come.

Travis pulled away from Pete and began to run the other way, blowing past Maxine as if she weren't there. Maxine was still standing there staring after Travis when Pete came up behind her.

Pete looked after Travis's spasmodically loping form. "Poor guy." Why was he feeling so sorry for him? Was it because Pete now knew the anguish that could lead someone to violence, knew how little the violence alleviated that anguish, that he felt for Travis now? He looked at Maxine, her face a potpourri of emotions. Poor Maxine.

"Come on," he said, resting a hand on her shoulder. She didn't move. She was staring past Pete at the diminishing shapes of Henry and Carlisle.

"How could she?" she asked.

"She's not herself," said Pete.

"You can say *that* again!"

"She's not her—"

Maxine whipped around and glared at him, her mouth a downward twist of I'm-too-old-for-your-goofy-humor kind of thing, but Pete's goofy humor had nothing to do with it. *She's not herself* rang around and rang between his ears, and suddenly everything about Ree began to make a certain ugly kind of sense.

110

# Chapter
# 12

Connie stood on her side of the half-opened door to her classroom and glared at the note in her hand. *How dare he!* The presence of Evelyn Smoot in her doorway six minutes before the bell . . . *six minutes before the bell!* He couldn't wait six minutes! It was police harassment of the most ugly sort, that was the only explanation for it. The note burned into Connie's brain. *The police chief would like a word with Henry,* it read; Connie scanned it, handed it back to Smoot coolly, oh so coolly, looked at the clock, and replied, "Okay. In six minutes." She couldn't call him out in front of the whole class that way, as if everyone wouldn't know just who had sent for him in less than the six minutes it would take for the bell to ring! Evelyn Smoot didn't argue. "Now," she said. Connie opened her mouth and looked at Smoot, hating her for knuckling under while at the same time recognizing in her level gaze that the principal was merely responding to another, higher authority. She shut her mouth without speaking and looked out over the class. For some reason, in that one-second examination of her students, they looked excruciatingly young to her, exceedingly vulnerable, unequivocally innocent, torn by the death of someone whom Connie was just beginning to understand had been more of a glue among them than they would ever know. But still, they all watched Connie with dread-filled, uncurious faces, as if knowing before she did exactly what the note had said. Anna Pease watched Connie in the same way she watched Travis, the new dynamics in the room having emboldened the usually reticent Anna to usurp the seat behind him. Travis Dearborn stared steadily at a spot halfway between Connie and Evelyn Smoot, oblivious to the worshipful eyes on his back. Kate McLellan raised a hand to cover a newly erupted pimple, in case, by some horrible luck, she was the one who would be called up front. Carlisle, and yes, Henry too, concentrated on the note still projecting stiffly from Connie's fingers. Even Alan Anderson raised his eyes from the near-to-popping top button on Natalie Price's vest and gripped the edge of his desk in what was meant to be a pantomime of tension, but looked to Connie like the real thing. Marty Sunderland stared hard at the floor as if afraid to be seen looking anywhere at all.

"Henry. Please."

And every one of them looked very carefully at everyone and anyone as long as it wasn't Henry himself.

Then something strange happened. Connie returned to her desk and dropped down into her seat. As she stretched her legs out underneath the desk, her shoe scuffed up against something, setting it rolling and clanking around on the floor. She peered under her desk, and somehow it didn't come as all that much of a surprise to her that she was looking at someone's class ring.

Once Connie had scooped up the ring so that it was visible, the room began to buzz as if it were full of locusts. Henry turned, almost out the door, and as he did so, Connie held out the ring to him. "Yours?"

But Alan Anderson was close behind. Henry's hand was too large for the ring, while Alan slipped it neatly onto his finger and picked up at once on the obvious theme. He bowed low before Connie.

"I'm your long lost prince! Or is it your ugly stepson?" He grabbed Connie's nearest hand and kissed it. The class let loose with gusts of relieved laughter that reminded Connie of the wind that followed a train. Connie, her eyes on Henry, shook Alan off as if he were a bothersome bee. When Henry left the room, Alan at once dropped her hand and his charade.

"I see," said Alan, "that we'd best continue this on some other occasion when Henry hasn't been arrested," and he peeled off down the row like a bomber plane that had just dropped its load on target.

Henry arrested!

That afternoon Connie stormed into the police station and past Jean at the desk without so much as glancing at the shelves she had put up with much trial and error that summer. She banged on the door of the chief's office and barely paused for the "What?" from the other side before charging in.

"Reasonable!" she hollered. "You call this reasonable? Hauling him out of school in the middle of the day and grilling him for hours in some stinking cell with the—"

"Oh, swell," said Willy, and he passed a hand over his face. It came out smiling. *Smiling*. Have a seat, Ms. Bartholomew. Please."

"I don't want a *seat*, I want an explanation! What was that line of bull you were shoveling last night about being reasonable, about needing facts, about—"

The chief stood up from behind the desk, no longer smiling. "There was no bull coming from my end of things last night. We spoke to Henry. It took"—he flipped over a thick wrist, looked at his watch, and then looked, again, at Connie, while she took the opportunity to resupply herself with air—"less than forty-five minutes. And we have no stinking cells. He agreed very readily to undergo a blood test, and we parted on amicable terms with no arrest or harassment or"—he looked hard at Connie—"verbal abuse."

"Oh really!"

"Really."

Connie slumped down into a chair, exhaled in frustration, and glared at the chief. Was there a certain gleam returning to his eye? Was it possible that he was actually seeing humor in something here? "I swear to God if you start laughing, I'll kill you," she said, and something about his face, as he tried to rearrange it into impassivity, made her almost burst out laughing herself. The chief sat back down behind his desk. "I just don't understand why you're picking on Henry. There are any number of other people you should be talking to instead of Henry, and all you—"

"In your opinion?"

"In my opinion!" she snapped. "Why is Henry the only one who has to have a blood test? I would imagine there are a few others around here capable of doing the job. And why, if you come down to that, do you insist on harassing only the students? Don't you think there are enough adults around who could have done it? Wouldn't an adult have more at stake if the truth came out that Bentley was knocked up? He'd lose his job! He'd get arrested!" Or would he? Connie tried to remember what she had learned about the age of consent.

"You have someone particular in mind?"

"No!" said Connie. "Of course not! I just want to know why you keep assuming that Henry, or a student at all, is responsible for Bentley's death."

The chief sighed. "First of all, let's assume that I should be talking to you about any of this anyway, okay? We'll assume that, okay? Second of all, I am not assuming anything else. We have the matter of a ring being found at the scene of the crime. We have the matter of two students missing rings—"

"One," Connie interrupted, then added reluctantly, "I just found Alan's under my desk. It was too small for Henry, but it fits Alan."

The chief received this new information with a short pause. "So. *One* particular student has lost his ring."

"It was stolen!"

The chief held up a hand. "We have the matter of an offhand remark made by yourself suggesting the fact that Bentley may have been interested in Henry or vice versa. We have the fact of Bentley's pregnancy by an unknown party who has elected not to come forward in a normal manner and discuss his involvement. We have a young man unable or unwilling to account for his time on the Saturday afternoon in question, and who has shown himself to be, on at least one occasion, preoccupied with the subject of murder."

Here the chief paused, and whether he did so purposely or not, the pause served to afford Connie an opportunity to examine just how much of this circumstantial evidence she herself had provided. She felt rotten.

The chief was watching her closely, and whatever he saw in her face seemed to cause him to veer off on an opposite tack. "Realizing, as I'm sure you do, that I can't exactly ignore the fellow, please don't forget that he has voluntarily agreed to the blood test, has consented to an appointment Friday afternoon for this purpose, and I can't see why he should do that unless he knows he has nothing to worry about. Wouldn't you agree?"

"Yes," said Connie at once. "I would agree."

The chief smiled at her. "Okay?"

"Okay," said Connie.

He looked at his watch. "I do have a few things to take care of before—"

Connie jumped up. "I'm sorry. I'm going."

The chief jumped up also. "I didn't mean to chase you out. I was going to say that if you gave me another two hours to straighten up a few loose ends, I would like very much to continue this someplace else." He gazed steadily into her eyes. "Or to continue onto something else."

Connie looked at her watch. It was only four o'clock, and if he did indeed finish up in two hours, it still gave them two more before she had to go out with Roy. They could meet for a drink. They could talk about things. She had a long evening ahead of her, and if she made things clear right up front, it would be all right, it would be more than all right, it would be something that she desperately needed.

"I have something to do later on, but if you do get through by six-thirty or so, you could come over for a drink, all right?"

"Six-thirty," said the chief, squinting at her.

Maxine Peck had waited so long to talk to Travis alone. She had followed him through the halls, she had stood outside his classroom, she had watched him in the gym, she had stayed late and waited for the last bus, the one on which the athletes rode at the end of practice, she had even followed him down the beach that day. Why? Oh, she knew that she was crazy about him, but there was something else, some other feeling, something that made how she felt about him seem so . . . noble! She felt a protectiveness toward Travis. *That Travis*. He was clearly misunderstood, by her mother, by Carlisle, probably by others, and it was up to Maxine to prove them wrong, to be loyal to her feelings, to be true to her adulthood, to break away from her childish past.

Maxine had many things she wanted to say to Travis, and one thing she wanted him to say to her. No, two things, really—the one that she had always assumed he would be able to say and the one that she knew, realistically, he would not. And then Wednesday it happened—he saw her standing outside the gym, peering through the door in just the way she had peered on many other days, but on this particular day something seemed to click between them. Instead of retreating through the wide doors at the opposite end of the gym that led to the lockers, he grabbed a towel he had thrown onto the front row of the bleacher seats, wiped his face and chest and underarms, slung it around his neck, and came straight toward her at the main gym doors. Maxine's heart began thrumming.

"Hey, Maxine." His face, his eyes, were solemn.

"Hi, Travis."

"What are you doing?"

"Watching you."

Something behind the eyes jumped, snapped, changed somehow.

"You do this a lot."

She nodded, unable to separate her tongue from her teeth.

"What for?"

"I . . . I want to talk to you."

"Oh yeah? What about?"

Maxine didn't want to have her conversation with Travis Dearborn begin and end right here.

"Could we go somewhere? I wanted to ask you about something. Alone." Travis looked around him, behind Maxine down the empty corridor, and then behind himself at the empty gym and the doors beyond. He spent some time with his back to her, and when he turned back, his eyes had changed expression. He shrugged.

Maxine knew that it was now or never. She had him wondering, she had his interest, it was possibly the only time in their lives that she would have his undivided attention, and she didn't want it to end in fifteen minutes in the hall outside the gym. "The Shack?"

Travis shook his head. "Can't. Game."

"Tomorrow, then?"

"Game. Besides, I don't go to the Shack much anymore."

"Friday. Between the buses then." Oh, it was a bold move! Between the buses was where you met when you weren't going to take the bus, when you were meeting a friend who had a car, or when you were walking somewhere together with someone, the Shack, for instance. Between the buses was in full view of those less fortunate kids who had nothing better to do than get on the bus and go home, and Maxine wanted to meet Travis there, wanted everyone to see her meet him, wanted them to see her walk off with him even if they only went around the corner and

117

back and not to the Shack at all. The big question was, would he agree?

Again Travis looked behind him at the empty gym, and back at Maxine; he narrowed his eyes and sighed. "Friday. Between the buses."

And suddenly Maxine didn't know whether to be ecstatically happy or despondently sad.

# Chapter
# 13

Pete pushed his cart through the produce row at the supermarket, his mind replaying sound bites that had been constantly flitting through his head since the altercation on the beach, while at the same time managing to shop for dinner for Ree and surface as needed to speak politely to the familiar faces that bobbed and weaved down the aisles before him. As he selected a head each of red and green garden lettuce, he though of the Browns, the two identical red heads, the two unique personalities inside. *She's not herself.*

"Hello, Pete."

"Hello." Pete paused before the citrus fruit while Alan Anderson's mother described in detail how much Alan had enjoyed Pete's sailing lessons the summer before.

"You just can't keep that boy off the water. It's fifty-four degrees out there on the Sound and what was he doing today? Sailboarding! Now, if only some of that water would wash away some of his fresh lip . . ."

The water had not washed away Bentley's eye shadow. Pete selected scallions and hand-picked a dozen cherry tomatoes from a basket and moved on toward the bakery section. Pete was only minimally interested in food—one-stop shopping or do without—but when he felt like it, he could get wrapped up in making a meal. His problem at present was that he wasn't quite sure he felt like it. At all. *I can't lose another one,* Ree had said. At the time Pete had assumed she had been referring to the loss, first, of a husband and then of a daughter, but now a whole new interpretation seemed to fit. What if the second daughter was at risk? Hadn't Carlisle hustled her out of the room the minute the outburst had been made? What would a mother do to protect her one remaining child, to keep from losing her to jail? What wouldn't she do?

Pete pushed past the fall apples and slowed his cart, selecting four fat Cortlands for baking with cream. Pink and cream. Hadn't Carlisle been wearing Bentley's pinks and creams of late? And Carlisle wasn't hanging around with Maxine these days. Bentley never had. Someone nudged his butt playfully with a shopping car and Pete whipped around.

"Well, if it isn't our little knight in shining armor," Elaine Carroll said, and Pete frowned. "Been consoling any grieving women of late, Pete? If only I'd known that was what it took, I'd have bumped someone off myself!" Pete stared at her. Elaine Carroll cocked one hip, flipped a dipping wave of chestnut hair out of her eyes, and smiled at him with a smile that really wasn't too nice.

"Hello, Elaine," he said, and tried to push on.

"Going home to suit up?"

Suit up. Travis Dearborn, crying on the road from the beach, coming from practice, but where was his gear? He'd been crying again, hadn't he, just before he had lit into Henry? Crying on that same beach where Bentley had died. But why would Travis Dearborn be crying over Bentley? Travis was in love with Carlisle. And wouldn't he know? Wouldn't the people most likely to see through the charade be the boyfriend and the mother? They must know! They had to know! And they were keeping it in, protecting the one remaining twin, attempting as best they could to carry on. That day in Bentley's room, that day when Carlisle had burst in, hadn't she said, "Keep out of *my* stuff?" Hadn't

Ree scrambled around to defuse her, hadn't she said while Pete waited outside, "Will you think what you're saying?" Hadn't she got them diverted onto Jimmy Solene, hadn't she insisted that Carlisle was not wearing Bentley's sweater when Pete had just seen it minutes before lying there on the bed? And then, right then, Ree must have noticed Pete watching Carlisle, gotten nervous, become afraid of him and of what he might have begun to figure out, and she had turned toward him and kissed him and . . .

Yes, Ree was very good at it, but Travis, Travis was not a man to fake his feelings, and the strain of pretended love for the shadow of his true love was breaking him in two, was breaking the "relationship" in two, was going to unravel the deception in the end. And hadn't Ree told him that Henry was more Bentley's type? Hadn't "Carlisle" been clinging to Henry and pushing away Travis ever since this all began? Ree was smart enough to pull this off, but was her daughter?

Smart. Connie had told him. Bentley was the smart one, but now Carlisle was beginning to do well in school . . .

Pete stopped pushing his cart at all and stood in the middle of the aisle in a turmoil of conjecture. Didn't it all make sense one way and one way only? Couldn't Bentley have longed for her sister's flashier life, her sister's superstar love? Couldn't she, the smart twin, the clever twin, have pounded her sister's head in on the beach, have switched clothes and makeup, gone home and waited for her sister "Bentley" to be found dead? She could fool them all with so little effort, she who knew her sister inside and out, she who would be expected to be "off" anyway, crushed with grief. She could fool them all, all but Travis, perhaps, and her own mother.

And *him*. He would have to talk to Willy. He would . . . Like a flash the image of Willy with the bottle of wine in his hand standing at the top of Connie's stairs snapped behind his eyes. No! He was damned if he was going to talk to Willy. At least not yet. Not until he was *sure* . . .

Pete snapped to, looked around, and found himself in the

middle of the cat food. He still had the main course to buy, and somehow he didn't think Tender Meaty Morsels were going to fill the bill. He headed for the meat counter. Ree liked red meat, he knew that much. He would grill a steak . . . Ree. And out of everything that suddenly made sense to Pete now, didn't Ree make the most sense of all? *Your friend, the police chief.* Wasn't that the big bonus, after all? Wasn't she trying not only to divert Pete but to secure Pete's goodwill, his compliance, his influence with his powerful friend? It was the only explanation that could account for her behavior toward him, after all. Ree. He didn't want to see her, and yet, suddenly, he did, now that he knew where he stood, now that he was wise to her game, now that he could play it himself. He selected an enormous short cut of the rump, feeling carnivorous. Now to the liquor store for a bottle of wine. Against his will, Pete found himself thinking of Pouilly-Fuissé. He hustled down the last aisle to the checkout, snagging his sneaker against the wheel of his cart in his haste. But no, it wasn't the wheel, it was something that was still rolling away lopsidedly. Pete bent down and scooped it up. This wasn't possible!

It was another class ring.

But this one bore this year's date.


He found Marty just coming out of the meat locker in back of the store. "Hey, Marty! This yours?" Pete held up the ring.

Marty's mouth fell open. He looked at the ring in Pete's hand, and he actually seemed about to shake his head no, but then he pushed at his bangs, blew air into his cheeks, looked behind him, then back at Pete, and then down at the ring.

"I just found this on the floor by the checkout. Just took a chance that yours was missing before I turned it in. Is it yours?"

"Yeah," said Marty. He reached out, snatched the ring from Pete's hand, and bolted back into the meat locker.

"Hey, Marty?"

"Thanks!" he hollered as he disappeared behind the door.

Pete shrugged. Something was wrong with *that* picture, too, but Pete was starting to think that so many things were wrong of late that *some* of it had to be in his mind.

Ree sat on the screen porch sipping a martini, watching Pete as he piled up the charcoal in an old stone fireplace just off to the left of the porch steps. It was six-thirty, and the air was uncharacteristically benign for Nashtoba at the end of September. Pete glanced up at Ree as she spoke, and had to admit that as the sky deepened into amber, her skin and hair took on a most flattering glow.

"I don't know," she was saying. "She was so upset when she came home today that I was almost afraid to talk to her. Something really has happened with Travis. She says she doesn't plan on seeing him anymore."

Pete said nothing, fussing unnecessarily with the coals, looking up, when he finally did so, not in her direction but over the marsh. It seemed to change daily, and this time of year it was at its most dramatic. But he knew every bend of its creek, every shade of its salt hay and sea goldenrod and asters; the marsh was infinitely more familiar to him than the woman on the porch. Still, he knew she was using him, he knew that much.

"I imagine if she and Travis are no longer seeing each other, there will be plenty of others to pick up the slack."

Ree gave a seemingly heartfelt sigh. "I wish I knew what to think about Henry. I am not all that comfortable with that situation right now, what with the chief questioning him so frequently and all. Sometimes he really does *seem* all right, and then every now and then I catch him watching her, watching me, as if we're all just parts of some big *plan* . . ."

Right, Pete thought, pin it on Henry, and then remembered that he himself had vindictively done the very same thing. "I thought you said that Henry was more Bentley's type."

Ree sat up in the rocker and peered through the screen at Pete. *"Did* I? I don't remember that." She got up out of the chair and pushed open the screen door, pointing her toes in their tan flats as she came down the stone steps, her matching tan wool slacks blowing against her thighs. She came up beside Pete and rested her fingers on the nape of his neck.

*Nice try!* Pete moved out from under her hand, picked up the bag of charcoal, and shook it. He wasn't going to be so easy *this* time. "You did say something about Coke-bottle lenses being more Bentley's thing?"

Ree shook her head, her eyes a fair imitation of puzzlement. "I tell you, I don't know what I'm saying these days. I think it's just as well that I'm seeing a psychotherapist. Did I tell you I was doing that?"

"No," said Pete, "you didn't," not sure that he wanted to be told about it now.

"Over on the Hook. He's been such a help. He warned me that this might happen, that Carlisle might seem to try to take her sister's place by taking on some of her interests as her own. Apparently it happens very often when a sibling dies, and he told me that with a twin, especially an identical twin, it could be ever so much more so."

Oh, sure, thought Pete, wouldn't that just explain away a few things very neatly! I mention that "Carlisle" is acting like "Bentley" and all at once you have a psychotherapist with theories to match!

Ree laughed self-consciously. "And I'm in danger of it myself, he said, trying to act young, trying to fill that spot that Bentley occupied; I think that in part accounts for my impulsive behavior of late." Ree looked at him, looked away, then looked back with more intensity.

"But I don't mean that completely, not really, Pete. I . . . I . . . You're a pretty special kind of guy, and all of a sudden the other night all my old rules didn't seem to mean a thing to me anymore. I didn't care what anyone thought,

I was afraid to wait to see what you were thinking, I just wanted to act on what *I* was thinking and feeling for once. Does that make any sense to you?"

"Perfectly," said Pete, doing nothing to take the bite of sarcasm down any. Pretty special kind of guy, right, Pete? The kind that women seem to like to run away from! Except, of course, for Ree . . .

Ree stared at him, her eyes seemingly puzzled.

"Of course, I still don't have the faintest idea what you're thinking." She laughed artificially. "And I thought only my daughters had that effect on me!" She laid soft fingers on his arm, just above his bandage. "Pete, does it bother you when I talk about her? About Bentley? I . . . I need to talk about her, and I don't really have anyone I can talk to about it. It's not fair to share my burdens with Carlisle, she has enough of her own."

"There's always Jimmy Solene," said Pete, and Ree snapped her fingers off his arm and stared at him with such a look of hurt surprise that all at once Pete felt a rush of guilt and confusion and doubt. "I'm sorry if that sounded rotten. He warned me off you, I—"

"Off *me?*" The incredulity seemed real enough. "You can't mean to tell me that the reason you hit him was because of—"

"I don't want to talk about Jimmy Solene," said Pete quickly. "I apologize for bringing it up. No, I don't mind you talking about . . . Bentley." And he looked at her quickly as he said it. She was still staring at him, and Pete could not make out if it was because of Jimmy or because of the hint of emphasis he had left on Bentley's name.

He pointed to her glass. "Another?"

Ree shook her head, still watching him. Pete took the empty from her and went inside for the steak.

They sat at Pete's pine table, which glowed soft yellow in the light of the hurricane lamp, and Pete watched Ree picking at her steak while he forgot about his own. She

125

drank very little of the wine, but Pete found that he was dipping down deep into the bottle as she talked on.

"Did you know that at the time I had the twins, it only happened once in eighty-six births?"

"What happened?"

"Twins. And out of all the twins born, only one quarter are identical. Did you know that?"

"I didn't." It was what he wanted, to talk about the twins, and to try to catch her out on some small thing that would prove to him that it was Bentley who was still alive. He would go to Willy with the solution to a case the chief had failed to solve, to be able to say to him that while Willy was wasting time with Connie, Pete was hard at work, succeeding on the chief's turf where the chief had failed. But was the chief succeeding on Pete's turf? Pete's *turf!* Pete shook his head. It was Connie's turf, and she could roll around on it with anyone she wanted, it had nothing to do with him.

"Pete? Are you all right?"

Pete gave himself a mental slap in the face and attempted to return to the woman before him. "It's fascinating," said Pete. "Twins."

"It's one single egg, Pete. They came out of one egg that divided into two different cell masses at some early stage and then turned into two people. Yes, it *is* fascinating, I can't stop thinking about it somehow, but after all the talk of twins gets done with, it really comes down to the same old thing: two individuals, two very different individuals, who in addition to all the problems the rest of us have, have to add a few more of their own by being twins. Of course, it's been fun for them, too, for all of us, I think, their being twins. It's just that . . . oh, I can't ever explain this to anyone right! The minute I try to explain how different they are, everyone starts in with those awful dichotomies! Which is the smart one? Which is the popular one? It isn't like that, and I hate it when they say things like that, I really do. If you hear things like that enough, you start believing it, *they* start believing it, and it isn't true, it

isn't that black and white! Why can't I make anyone understand that just because when the two of them are together,
Carlisle is doing most of the talking, that doesn't make her
the only personality of the pair? You should hear Bentley
when Carlisle's not around! And just because Bentley gets
better grades doesn't mean she possesses the only brain for
both of them! They aren't halves, they're wholes!''

Pete felt a momentary guilt, remembering his own mus-
ings about the clever one, the popular one, but the guilt was
soon erased by pain as he remembered what Ree seemed to
have forgotten, that they weren't a "they" at all anymore,
that one of them was dead. One of them, yes, but which
one? And wasn't this a very convenient conversation for
Ree to be having with him? Wasn't this supposed to explain
why Carlisle wasn't acting like Carlisle at all?

"But let's be realistic. We both know how fast a person
gets forgotten, don't we? How long will it be before I forget
some special thing, something Bentley once said that was
so treasured, some expression she used to have, some . . .''
Ree turned her head away and swallowed. Silence fell.

Pete leaned toward her, immediately sorry that she had
now remembered one of her daughters was dead after all.
"It must have been difficult raising twins," he prompted,
but he was no longer speaking on behalf of his own theories, he was asking only because it was all he could offer
to help her bring her daughter back, to stave off a little
longer the fear that her daughter would be forgotten. Ree
responded with a smile, and charged off at once on this
new course.

"Of course, I read everything I could get my hands on
about twins once I had them, and I did all those things they
suggested—I kept Car's hair short and left Bentley's longer,
I dressed them differently, we tried to do something special
individually with each of them as much as we could." She
paused, and Pete guessed that she was now assessing
whether her efforts had been a success or a failure. Yes, it
must have been hard to be a twin sometimes, but how hard
it must have been to be their only parent! But Ree said it

had also been fun, for all of them, and maybe it was time for her to think about that.

"Could you always tell them apart?" he prompted.

"At first. It was strange, really, because as babies, they were different weights and even had different-shaped faces, and were quite easy to tell apart; then as they got a little older, they began to look more and more alike. And the funny part was that once they got *much* older, they seemed to *want* to look more alike! I never put them in the same outfit on the same day, but they started doing it themselves, and one day Carlisle took the scissors to Bentley's hair and just about butchered it. I can still see her head now. And of course, then it had to come off shorter when the hairdresser fixed it and they ended up with these matching curly red mops of hair and they were absolutely thrilled with it. Every time I turned around, they would set in trying to fool me." Ree smiled and ran a finger around the rim of her wineglass. Her eyes were wet, but no tears fell.

"So they *could* fool you?"

"Never for long. Hardly a minute, not if I were concentrating. They really were so different in so many ways. Carlisle's face was never still; Bentley had a look in her eyes that could tell you worlds were going on behind them. But it really is odd, twins—identical ones, I mean. They had all the same diseases at the same time, they both cut their teeth at just the same time in just the same order, they both needed the same types of braces, their IQs were the same . . . No, I could tell them apart when they were talking and moving and acting like themselves; it was just when they set out to fool me on purpose. The trick was to catch me with a roast half out of the oven or my arms full of laundry or while I was chasing the dog. Those were the times that it worked, Carlisle coming up to me and pointing at Bentley and saying something like, "Carlisle has a sore throat," and seeing if I caught them out. It was always Carlisle's face that gave it away first, of course; she couldn't keep a straight face for two seconds, I swear. They had a lot of fun trying to fool other people, though, and

I'm afraid they were a little better at it than was entirely good for us all.'' She stopped talking. Her finger stopped moving on the glass. She raised her eyes to Pete's, eyes that had turned tawny in the yellow light, and Pete could think of nothing but the pain in them, spilling over now into golden wet tears.

"Ree." He pushed back his chair, stood up, moved toward her.

"I'm so sorry. I can't help it. They were so close to each other, this is going to kill Carlisle, I swear it is. She adored her sister, she never wanted to go anywhere without her, she'll be so lost! Lost!" Ree pushed against her own chair, struggled to her feet, and dashed a hand across her tears.

She seemed on the verge of collapse, and Pete reached out to her, but as she turned in to him, he began to wonder if he had after all imagined it. Her face was now all flashing white teeth and shining wet lips, and the soft turquoise of her sweater's fullest parts pressed against him. "Oh, Pete," she said, raising her mouth in a way that told him she very much wanted him to kiss her, and suddenly Pete wanted to kiss her very much, wanted to go to bed with her, wanted to stay with her this time.

"Ree," he said again, then nothing more.

# Chapter
# 14

Connie was beginning to think that there was something in the atmosphere that was conspiring to fill her apartment with multiples of men. Why the hell couldn't one of them ever do what he said he was going to when he said he was going to do it? Six-thirty, she had said, goddammit! And why was it always this stupid, fat-ass cop who kept barging in here when he was least expected and least welcome? Not that she wouldn't have ordinarily been grateful for anyone and anything that interrupted Roy in his obnoxious opening gambit, which Connie was sure she had a good twenty minutes more to suffer through when Willy knocked on the door, but somehow she found the whole situation so embarrassing, the stupid, edgy look on Roy's face so irritating, Willy's unreadable squint so *infuriating*.

"I told you I had something to do later," Connie snapped at him. "You think I was lying? It's eight-fifteen and we're going out."

"Hey!" Willy held up both hands in surrender but continued to squint at Roy. "Don't shoot me. I thought I'd stop by, just in case. I got held up, it happens."

Roy Millis said nothing.

"You're . . . ?"

"Roy Millis," Connie snapped out. "Chief McOwat. He

seems unable to turn around without my constant contributions to the details of this case."

Still Roy didn't speak, and since the chief didn't offer a hand, he didn't offer one either.

"Don't wait up," said Connie, and she gave Roy a little shove toward the stairs.

"A moment," said Willy behind her. There was something insistent about his hand on her thinly covered arm, and Connie didn't respond very well to insistence. She yanked herself away, stepped back, waved him before her. "Just go, please," she said, furious with him for being so late, furious with Roy for being there at all, furious with herself for having ever said yes to this stupid, ridiculous evening. She determined to make it a short one.

But she was a little miffed to find that all of a sudden Roy seemed to want to make it a short one also.

Two hurried ales and one rotten steak later, she was back at her doorstep, watching Roy's red Trans Am pull away from the curb. Soon after she was further miffed to see the chief's red and white Scout come to life down the street and pull away also. What was he doing, watching to see what time she got home from her date? She was so annoyed that for a fleeting instant she almost wished she had stayed out later.

# Chapter
# 15

Rita arrived at Factotum at eight o'clock the next morning, eyebrow-deep in her usual reams of worry over Maxine. The thing of it was, she had seemed better today—she had hopped out of bed on time, had spent less than her usual hour and thirty minutes in the bathroom, and had come out looking less glued and pale. She had eaten an almost normal breakfast of a container of yogurt and a glass of juice, she had even said good-bye to her mother. Something was *wrong*.

Rita stepped out of her car and began her usual morning ritual of picking up the newspaper from the step, pushing open the door, turning on the lights, collecting whatever was left lying on couch or chairs from the day before, spreading out the newspaper on her desk for a read. The phone rang. "Factotum."

"Oh! Hello, Rita. This is Ree. Ree Brown. Is Pete there?"

Rita looked at the clock. He *should* have been there. "Hang on. I'll see." She clipped down the hall to the door that opened into Pete's kitchen and knocked. No answer. She pushed open the door and peeked in, and raised her eyebrows at what she saw.

Two plates of picked-at steak and salad, a half-full basket

of bread, two wineglasses, one empty and one nearly full, one of the antique kitchen chairs tilted at a crazy angle against the wall and the other pushed out into the middle of the room. Rita looked at the closed door at the end of the kitchen that led into Pete's bedroom–living room and was just about to make a quick retreat when the door burst open and Pete's naked upper torso leaned out.

"Rita?"

"Correct. Please excuse my presence. Ree's on the phone."

Given the state of the kitchen, she was not prepared for the look of wild panic that flashed across Pete's face. "Tell her I'm asleep, will you, Rita?"

Rita stared at him. His hair was rumpled up into spikes, his chin covered with stubble, his eyes dark-ringed and haunted. He looked, thought Rita, almost exactly as bad as Maxine had looked better. Something was definitely *wrong*.

Sarah Abrew watched Pete hop around her living room from couch to windowsill to coffee table, crumpling up her morning paper in his good fist, jabbing the fingers that protruded from the cast into his still wet hair until he looked like a porcupine. Finally she could stand it no longer. *"Lordy,* will you set and stay set!" she hollered.

Pete whipped around and looked at her with hurt surprise.

"Either that or get on out of here," she grumbled. "You're indigesting my cream of wheat!"

Pete crossed back over to the couch and threw himself down on it full length. "Oh Christ, Sarah, I don't know what's wrong with me! I think I'm overtired."

It was just the sort of self-absorbed, hypochondriacal remark that he almost never made, and Sarah narrowed her dimming eyes at him with concern. "Aren't you sleeping?" she asked, and a half-sheepish, half-pleased-with-himself flash of something shot across his face. She sighed. The man was such an open book, thought Sarah, that she could not for the life of her understand why his ex-wife had so much trouble figuring him out.

Pete pulled up in front of the Nashtoba Ladies' Library, yanked on the emergency brake, and sat there contemplating the dashboard of his truck. The Nashtoba Ladies' Library was so named because it had been started back in the mid-1800s by a group of sea captains' wives, and although a more forward-thinking newcomer suggested at town meeting every now and then that they "update" the name, after hot words from the purists, it was always voted down. The name of the library was the Nashtoba Ladies' Library, Eva Chase, the librarian, annually concluded, and that was the end of that—until the next year and the next meeting. Every month or so an irate tourist demanded to know why men couldn't use the library and was soon straightened out. It was, Pete thought, a small price to pay, if a price it was at all. He had a sneaking suspicion that Eva Chase got most of her excitement out of these occasional confrontations with irate males.

And so what was *he* doing here, anyway? Was a mind in turmoil naturally drawn here in search of answers from books? Pete doubted very much that the kind of answers he needed would be contained within the four colonial yellow walls in front of him, and he sat some minutes longer contemplating the beauty of the nearly two-hundred-year-old buttonwood tree out front before coming to grips with just what question he was actually asking. *Was* she using him? He had woken to find her gone. At first he had felt great regret at finding himself alone, but the regret was soon followed by relief. She had already called Factotum twice this morning. Of course she was using him. Why else would she be behaving like this? He slammed the truck door harder than it could probably stand, and went inside.

The Ladies' Library was little changed from the days when the ladies first founded it, with the exception of the books contained within. A huge teak desk that had come across the ocean on one of the whaling vessels was still perched exactly in the center of the room with a hand-lettered cardboard sign that read "desk." The ceilings were high and vaulted, the floors worn and creaking, and many of the books were flaking their pages but still holding their own along with the plastic-coated new ones by their side.

Twins. The card index was pathetically small, and after he skated over the many references to "Twain," he found only two meager references to twins. One was fiction and the other was biography, and he went in search of the biography in hopes that other twins would shed some light on these particular twins, but the biography was not on the shelf. Pete next turned to the encyclopedia and looked under "twins." Twin Falls: city, pop. 1970 21,914. The Twins: English name for Gemini, a constellation. Twins: See "multiple births." Pete turned to "multiple births" and learned, again, a few of the things that Ree had told him. In addition he learned that identical twins have different fingerprints, but that didn't help in a situation where prints had never been taken in the first place, and he very much doubted that in this case any printing had ever been done. He learned that identical twins had the same blood group types. Did that mean that whatever testing was done to determine the father of the fetus, the mother could still be either Bentley or Carlisle?

Pete closed the book. None of this information helped him at all in trying to determine if Bentley could be fooling them all, nor did it help to answer Pete's question of whether Ree was using him to help perpetrate this farce, but it did help him to understand some of Ree's mystic wonder over the uniqueness of each of her daughters. Pete returned the encyclopedia to the shelf, paused a minute to speak with Eva Chase, and left, feeling on the one hand the need for a long, soul-searching chat with Willy, and on the other, never wanting to see the man again.

It was 3:45 when Pete returned to Factotum, and as he pulled up to his house, he found not only that Henry, Carlisle, and Maxine had arrived off the bus as expected, but that Alan Anderson and Marty Sunderland had unloaded

outside his door as well. Maxine was standing in the doorway, watching but not participating, and the three boys
were grouped around Carlisle, performing as only three
seventeen-year-old males around a newly unattached female can. Pete looked closer and changed his mind. Alan
Anderson was performing. Henry was watching, with nothing more than the intense blinking behind his glasses to
betray what he might be thinking about the scene. Marty
Sunderland appeared to be totally indifferent to Carlisle's
presence, his every move and posture indicative of an
impatience to be gone.

"Hey!" said Carlisle, if indeed it really was Carlisle.
"It's the boss! C'mon, guys, leave me alone and let me
get to work!" She sounded, thought Pete, quite a bit less
interested in getting back to work than she was in talking
to these three, and Pete felt an unreasonable resentment
toward her. Travis was barely cold! As if a director had
summoned all the actors to move on to the next scene, the
three young men altered course. Alan stopped talking but
didn't move, waiting and watching for someone else to do
so first; Henry took one step closer to Carlisle and didn't
budge; Marty Sunderland flipped at his bangs with a still
ringless hand and shuffled toward the road, giving Pete a
much wider berth than seemed necessary.

Of course, a person might not want to wear a ring that
no longer bore his correct year. Of course, he might not
order another ring that *did* bear the correct year, having
already been burned once . . . But there was something
fishy about all these rings floating around. If one were lost
on the beach in the middle of a murder, and the murderer
wanted to replace it . . .

"Yo! Al!" Marty hollered. "Let's go! C'mon!" He
jerked an elbow in the direction of the beach, and Pete
wondered how much money he could make if he put up a
toll booth.

Alan looked at Henry. "You coming?"

"I work here," said Henry, not a muscle twitching in his
entire face.

Alan laughed, and to Pete the sound seemed to contain about nine-tenths skepticism and one-tenth envy. Alan walked up to Carlisle, scooped her into a ballroom dance pose, dipped her to within a foot of the grass, and sprang her back to her feet, laughing. And didn't she cling to him just a second too long? Apparently Pete wasn't the only one to think so. Henry, who had watched and blinked and watched and blinked again, now made what seemed to Pete to be a very cold-blooded strategic move, if taken in the greater scheme of things. He turned to Pete.

"I'm to the point of hanging the Meechams' shutters, a procedure which I believe would go much more smoothly if it were treated as a two-man job. I don't believe"—here he looked pointedly at the bulky contraption fastened to Pete's hand—"that you would be a functional addition to a team. Would it be acceptable if I brought Maxine along?"

Carlisle's face began to glow red.

"Sure," said Pete. "If she wants to."

"Sure!" said Maxine, and she dashed inside, where through the open door Pete could see her having a surprisingly sedate discussion with her mother. Rita was smiling at her! Maxine was smiling back?

"Excuse me," said Henry in Pete's ear. "If I could have a brief word?"

"Sure," said Pete, glancing at Carlisle; she was watching Henry while attempting to appear not to be doing so. Henry took Pete by the elbow and guided him a safe distance off.

"I'm afraid I will not be here tomorrow afternoon as expected, due to this matter of the blood test. Perhaps you've heard about the blood test?"

Pete shrugged and nodded in what he hoped was a vague semicircular direction.

"The test, if I recall correctly what the chief has explained to me, could eliminate completely any possibility of me being the father of Bentley's child, which, it so happens, I am not." When he had concluded this unusual speech, Henry gazed through his glasses at Pete without blinking, without giving evidence of any emotion at all.

Was it possible he could be so little rattled by all this ugliness? Was this the guy Connie thought was so caring, so warm, so . . .

Pete stared at Henry's thick lenses and began to feel a little irked. "Well, then, there's nothing to worry about, is there? They'll stick you with a needle, hover over your blood for a few days or weeks or whatever, and then, assuming you're eliminated, I suspect they'll abandon you in search of a more likely killer. And don't worry about Factotum. If it appears we might be able to get some work out of Maxine two days running, I can have her fill your place. Temporarily, of course. Unless it becomes necessary to do anything on a more permanent basis, of course."

Henry blinked at Pete. "I take your meaning," he said, and Pete felt suddenly and sickeningly rotten, mean, and childish, far more childish than this seventeen-year-old boy. He opened his mouth to apologize, but Henry had moved toward the door of Factotum, halted, and turned around. "And don't *you* worry about Factotum. If you feel you've reached the age where you should stick to the more administrative tasks on a permanent basis, Maxine or Carlisle or I could fill your place."

If it weren't for those glasses, thought Pete, I really do think I might belt him. Or was it *because* of those glasses, because those glasses kept flashing reminders of Glen Newcomb in his face? Pete watched Henry blinking away behind them, looking many things, but courteous and polite weren't among them.

No, it wasn't just because of the glasses.

# Chapter
# 16

When Connie arrived at the teachers' parking lot unusually
soon after the bell, there was Alan Anderson sitting on the
tiny hood of her car and tossing an apple in the air. He
would, she thought, have to have that apple, and he would,
she knew, somehow manage to hand it over to her without
actually stating the joke out loud, but still she hoped he
wasn't going to overproduce it. No. He saw her, flipped
the apple over his head into the open car and pushed himself off it, his whole face and body uncharacteristically taut.

"I thought you guys never bugged out at the bell," he
said to her, his smile stretching too tight and too short and
retreating too fast into a clenched jaw.

"I thought you guys weren't supposed to hang around
out here," she answered him, waving a hand at random at
the various cars still cramming the teachers' lot, implying
with the gesture that many of her cronies were obviously
still hard at work, but Alan didn't seem to catch it. He
made an impatient sound that seemed to dismiss her role
as a person who played by the rules, and something about
the sound, and his stance as he stood beside her car, made
her stop and go no closer. This is ridiculous, she told herself. She wouldn't be feeling this foolish if Willy McOwat
hadn't filled her head with thoughts of one of these guys

bashing in Bentley's head, and she still wouldn't be standing here like an imbecile five feet away from her own car if the particular student in front of her hadn't at one point lost his ring. And still, thinking all this, she found herself even less able to move. Alan Anderson noticed that she stopped, and took in her look; there was nothing about it that he didn't seem to see and read and understand, and all at once she was filled with an old, familiar, yet poorly defined feeling of having let the team down.

"Well, if it isn't the light of my life," said Roy Millis behind her.

Connie whirled around, but not fast enough to miss the change of focus in Alan's eyes, or the cold contempt that filled them.

"Slumming, are we?" asked Roy, and Connie, looking into the eyes of the teacher, whipped around to face Alan, suddenly clearly aware of what she had just done, what she had failed to give him. A ring lost, a ring found . . .

But Alan was gone, disappearing around the corner of the clapboard school building, heading toward the woods. Behind her, Connie heard Roy's voice saying, "We have to talk, my love, oh *boy* do we have to talk."

"Oh, please," snapped Connie, suddenly afraid of Roy too, not of his actual physical presence as she had been with Alan, but of what he now represented to her—her last chance to beat an afternoon's aloneness. She jumped into her car, slammed the door, cranked the key, ground into gear, and spun out of the lot.

As she drove down Shore Road, trying not to think about Alan and Roy, the next student that she saw was Anna Pease walking along the sandy shoulder. Connie slowed down to offer Anna a ride, but Anna refused it with a shake of her head. It seemed apt, in keeping with Connie's own feelings of failure.

And they weren't through with her yet. Connie stopped at the supermarket and wasn't even halfway down the produce row when Marty Sunderland and his father rounded the front of her cart and blocked her path.

"Hey!" said Marty's father, a large, puffy pink man whose name Connie could not, at the moment, recall, as he seemed, at the moment, not to be able to recall hers, unless it was just that he was the last remaining person on Nashtoba who didn't want to embarrass her by calling her Mrs. Bartholomew.

"What's going on with the kid here? He's no dumbbell; why are his grades going to the devil all over again? I want to know what's going on here!"

Connie tried to remember just what had been wrong with Marty's last paper, but for some reason all she could remember was Henry Tourville's GOVUTER and the blow torch, and the chief sitting in her living room with Carlisle's blank page in his hand. It had struck her as wrong, that paper from Carlisle, that poor show of self-esteem from one of the school's queens.

Connie looked at Marty, who was looking anywhere and everywhere but back at her, standing as far away from his father as he could get. "This isn't a very good place to get into it, Mr. Sunderland." Marty's head swung around and then quickly away again, but not before she saw the flash of relief. She continued, but now she spoke directly to Marty. "Let me go over your work and your records, Marty, and we can get together next week. You can lay out your plans for me and we can see what needs to be done, okay?"

"Okay," said Marty's father.

"Okay, Marty?" Connie asked, as if his father hadn't spoken.

Marty took a minute to assimilate the fact that he was being addressed. "Okay," said Marty, and Connie, now feeling heavy with fatigue, shoved off with her cart.

On Friday morning Connie's fatigue was still persistent, and the absence of Henry Tourville and Alan Anderson in the after-lunch history class didn't help. On the one hand, Alan's, she felt a guilty relief; on the other she felt an equally guilty fear. Henry had a lab test that afternoon, and it was important, crucially so, that he appear for it. The appearance alone was of more significance even than the test. If Henry failed to show for the test, what conclusion would the police chief jump to, the one to which she had unwittingly half pushed him?

"Where's Henry?" she asked the class casually. She watched the remaining ten heads swivel left and right, watched eyes widen and narrow. Carlisle, Connie noticed, seemed very pale, either because she was very pale or because the new makeup she was wearing made her skin appear all that much whiter beneath the streaks of mauve blush and blue shadow. Did she know where Henry was? Did they all know? What *did* they know? Something, Connie was sure, and she was shot through with a fierce and quick impatience with the roomful of raging hormones with which she had to deal. Why the hell couldn't they just say what was on their minds? Why couldn't they sort themselves out and stay sorted, leaving her out of it?

At the end of the class Connie could stand it no longer—she closeted herself in the phone booth at the back of the teachers' room and called Henry's home.

Henry Tourville's mother was an artist, and in Nashtoban terms, a successful one. The Artful Dodger Gallery near the dock sold every watercolor that she could supply, and if by chance she ran to excess, there were several places on the Hook eager to take them off her hands. If she was home alone, Connie knew that the odds were fifty-fifty that she would pick up the phone. If the particular work was going well, she would answer; if it wasn't, she would avoid all contact with the outside world. Henry's father, a marine biologist, worked off-island at the Coastal Studies Institute.

"Hello," said Henry's mother.

"This is Connie Bartholomew," said Connie, envisioning a distracted hand dribbling a mud-colored blob of paint onto an otherwise pearly and perfect sky. "I'm sorry to bother you . . ." Now she was sounding like a cop! "But I was concerned about Henry. Is he all right?"

"Henry? Is this the Institute?"

Connie gave her time to withdraw from the dunes or whatever else it was that she was painting and tried not to sound impatient. Connie wouldn't be calling about Henry Senior, her husband. Connie was her *son's* teacher, for God's sake! "Henry's teacher. Connie Bartholomew. Henry *Junior*. He wasn't in class . . ."

"He wasn't? Why not?"

"I don't know. He—"

"He left for school on the bus. I saw him. He looked straight back at me from the top of the hill and waved. Are you sure you haven't just missed him somehow?"

She made it sound as if Connie had misplaced him, misfiled him, failed to recognize the long stalk of his straw-topped body in the crowd. "He must have missed my class for some reason. I assumed he wasn't in school, that he had stayed home sick. I'm sorry to have bothered you," she said again, not wanting to alarm her unnecessarily, but she found herself unable to let it go at that. "As far as you know, has he kept his plans regarding the appointment at the lab?"

Henry's mother remained silent for a moment, a moment that told Connie she was fully returned from her dunes and was fully aware of the turn the conversation was taking. "His father is going to meet him here at three-thirty," she answered finally, the voice that had until now continued to sound partially absent taking on a fully present and anxious twang. "They leave from here for the lab. Something *is* wrong?"

"Not at all. It was foolish of me to call you. I only needed to speak with him before Monday about a paper of his, and since he is obviously here in school after all, I'll just track him down in the halls."

"He shouldn't have missed your class," said Henry's mother, and something about her tone told Connie that having made that pronouncement, the subject was dispensed with, the dunes or the sea or whatever-it-was that she was putting on paper was back in control. Perversely, where

143

before Connie had not wanted to distract her, now she felt that Henry deserved a little more of her concern.

Henry was not in the building. Somehow Connie knew this, could feel it. Still, she went to the principal's office to check on the attendance of the day, walked through the wide-open door and up to the desk that sat jammed against the wall in what she always thought of as the forecourt— the spacious room behind the door to the right of it enclosing Evelyn Smoot, the queen. The school secretary, Justine Beamish, no older than Connie and yet already the possessor of a frayed and graying braid, pushed at the braid with one hand and shuffled the notes on her desk with the other in response to Connie's request. "Henry Tourville. Henry Tourville. I know I saw something . . ."

"Absent," called Evelyn Smoot, emerging from her office. "Is something wrong? His father called just after eight. He has the bug. It was when you were fiddling with the coffee, Justine, I left you a note."

"Nothing's wrong," said Connie, but something was, and somehow Connie knew that Evelyn at least, if not Justine, now knew it. Surely Henry's mother hadn't lied to her about Henry, so just as surely, Henry's father hadn't placed any A.M. call. Who had? Henry? Was he good enough at impersonating his father to have gotten by Evelyn Smoot's discerning ears?

After the junior U.S. history class, Connie monitored a short study hall that contained representatives of the three higher grades. Carlisle Brown was in it, Travis Dearborn was in it, Kate McLellan was in it. Connie looked around. Travis was in his customary seat near the window, but Carlisle was not on the other side, a fact that didn't much surprise Connie, considering the various ups and downs of late. As she looked around the room, she couldn't find Carlisle at all. What was going on around here? Was this some new open-door policy, notice of which Connie had somehow missed? Carlisle had been there the class before. Connie had noticed her specifically because of her paleness.

Had she become ill and gone home? Connie just had time at the end of the study hall to scoot past the nurse's office, but Carlisle was not and had not been there. The hell with it.

Connie managed not to think further about Carlisle or Henry until the last class of the day. She was discussing with the sophomores, or attempting to discuss with the sophomores, what exactly was so dark about the Dark Ages, and she was watching Maxine as she spouted off. All of a sudden Maxine's eyes, which had been trained dreamily off into space, came sharply into focus, and Connie followed their tracks out the window just in time to see Travis Dearborn slipping into the woods. What the hell was going on around here, Skip Day a year and six months early? Henry fakes sick, Alan never shows, Carlisle disappears, Travis bolts not a half hour later? Wasn't this a school? Weren't there such things as *rules?*

Connie realized that now both she and Maxine had begun watching the clock, and Connie had little doubt where Maxine planned to go at the sound of the bell. Connie planned to go straight to the Tourvilles' to see if Henry had showed up to meet his father for the test. If Henry showed up, there would be no need to worry. If Henry showed up, it would mean Henry was not worried about the test, and if Henry wasn't worried about the test, then Connie didn't have to worry about it. But what if Henry didn't show up? What if he didn't come home? What would the chief think? He'd think Henry had bolted.

Connie watched the clock, and she watched Maxine watch the clock, and the longer she watched Maxine watch the clock, the more concerned she began to get about other things as well. When the bell finally sprung them, Connie found herself rooted to the spot. She turned from the clock to the window. She waited. She watched. She saw what she expected to see—Maxine Peck hustling around the corner of the building and into the woods right at the spot where Travis had entered, right where Alan had gone the day before. What the hell was in there but woods? Connie tried to remember where the woods came out, what was in there along the way, what the big attraction could be, but she couldn't concentrate on it, couldn't keep her mind off Henry and the test. She packed her things into her canvas tote and steamed out of the building and off to the Tourvilles' with every expectation of finding what she wanted to find, the two Henrys about to leave for the lab.

The Tourvilles' house was much what one would expect an artist and a marine biologist to compromise upon—the white porch railing was lined with bronze chrysanthemums that trapped the sun and shadow and intrigued the eye, but as Connie crossed its neat, enameled floor to the door, she could see the piles of rubber tubing in the corner, and through the window she saw a fish tank full of logy, crusty marine specimens that any artist would have a hard time calling scenic. Connie knocked at the door, but when Henry's mother answered, she didn't have to ask any questions to figure out just what was going on. A graying blond man not as tall as Henry but with thicker glasses was just hanging up the phone at the table in the hall, his face tight with worry. He spoke to his wife, both of them oblivious to Connie in the door.

"I don't pretend to understand it," Henry Senior said, in a voice that Henry Junior could have imitated with only a minimal drop in register. "He has not, it appears, arrived at the lab on his own, nor has he communicated with them in any fashion. They are expecting him today. Now."

Connie looked from one Tourville face to another and saw the fear flash between them.

# Chapter
# 17

Pete sat on the back stoop and stared out over the marsh, trying to absorb some strength from it, trying to absorb some motivation, trying to get up and get moving and stop *dwelling* on things so much. It was working so poorly and he was so deep in his obsessive musing that he didn't even hear Ree approaching until she spoke to him a foot from his ear.

"Rita said you were back here moping. I hope it's not something I've said?"

Pete looked up and was immediately blinded, first by the light behind her head, and then by the artificiality of her smile.

"I'm looking for Carlisle," she said.

Pete slid over on the cold stone stoop, and even though he didn't look at her at all, it seemed to be enough for her; she sat.

"Listen, Pete. I don't do these things very well. You haven't called me, so I decided to just come over here and have this thing out. I'm not looking for Carlisle. Well, I am looking for Carlisle, but once I got here and Rita said she wasn't here, I decided that I had to face up to it one way or the other. I had to talk to you. I understand if you don't want to see me, if I'm not your type, I really do understand if you think we're getting too involved or—"

Pete jumped up off the stoop. How much of a sucker could one person be? God only knew how many times she had called him, and now she had arrived at his door wanting to "have it out"! It was not possible that she could be wanting him this much; only a fool would be expected to believe in all this. He felt the cold clutch of a plot brewing. He was not going to fall for this, he wasn't! But he turned and looked down at her, sitting alone on the stoop, hugging her knees, looking small and crushed and miserable, and somehow the things that began to spew out of his mouth were not at all the things he had planned to say.

"It's not true. All those things you think I'm thinking, none of it's true. At least I don't think it is. I'm not any good at this either. I—"

"Pete!" someone hissed from behind the screen of his porch. It was Rita. "You have another visitor. You'd better come in here for this one."

"Oh, for God's sake, Rita!" said a second voice that Pete still knew too well, and Connie barged past Rita, snapped the screen door into Ree's backside, and sailed out between them onto the lawn.

Pete stared at her. She was still in what must have been her teaching clothes—a pair of khaki-colored corduroys, a fisherman's sweater, tan moccasins on her feet. Her hair was held back in a gold clip, and the shine of her hair and the shine of the clip were equal; she seemed to be gold all over. She looked much as she always had, with one notable exception; it seemed unlikely to Pete, but there again, Pete knew Connie's every expression, and it was very clear that right now she was afraid.

"What's the matter?" Pete asked her, and heard his own voice struggle with, and fail to achieve, indifference.

"Is Henry here?"

Henry again!

"Henry's off getting a lab test. He's not coming in today."

Connie walked away from them, turning her back on them, and Pete could tell that she was struggling to remain calm. He moved up quickly behind her, almost touching her before he remembered that it was not a very good idea, yet succeeded in turning her around with a tone he knew had now traveled light-years away from indifference. "What's the matter?"

She whirled around, blinking furiously. "He's gone. He didn't come to school, he faked a call from his father, he didn't meet his father to go for the test, he's not at the lab. He didn't show up at the lab. He's bolted. I can't think why he's bolted, I know he didn't do it, I can't imagine him taking off this way, but I know what it looks like, I know what Willy's going to think it looks like! This is all he'll need! He'll call in the state police, they'll have the helicopters out on a manhunt! I have to talk to him, I have to get him to show up for the test before Willy finds out. I need to—"

"Wait a minute."

"Don't you see what Willy will think? Don't you get it? Henry's gone! He wrote that stupid paper that I showed to the chief. His ring is still missing. The chief thinks he was mucking around with her. The only reason he believes him at all is because he agreed to the test! He told me right out it was his only proof of innocence! He's going to arrest him."

"Wait a minute here. Wait." Pete held his fingers in front of her lips as she opened her mouth to cut him off, but again he was careful not to touch her. He was also careful to keep some of what he was thinking from reaching his eyes, since some of what he was thinking had to do with the apparent fall from grace of the police chief now that he had set off after her precious Henry Tourville. "I spoke to Henry about this. He was all set to have the test; I distinctly remember him saying that he was definitely not the baby's father, and agreeing with me that the test was a good idea so that then the police would leave him alone and start looking elsewhere for who killed Bentley. He must have mixed up the day." But even as Pete saw the disbelief in Connie's eyes, he felt it in his own. Henry had begged off work for the purpose of taking the test. If he had forgotten the test, he'd have shown up for work. He wouldn't miss an opportunity to be here with Carlisle unless he . . . Carlisle. *Rita said Carlisle wasn't here.* Pete couldn't believe he had been so preoccupied with his own troubles that he had failed to realize the significance of the fact that Carlisle had not shown up for work either.

As if reading his thoughts, Connie continued. "I thought maybe he was with Carlisle and just forgot the time. Carlisle disappeared from school this afternoon in the middle of the day. I was planning to stop at her house next . . ."

"She isn't there," said Pete, and only then, only because he was now remembering that Ree had pretended to come here looking for Carlisle, which meant Carlisle wasn't at home, did he remember Ree. He turned around to speak to her, but the stoop, the porch, the entire lawn was empty.

"I have to find him," said Connie. "I have to find Henry before Willy does, I have to talk to him to get him to come back on his own. Carlisle is probably with him."

"I don't think so," said Pete, whose mind had suddenly clicked on, who was now fitting together the last few remaining pieces of relevant conversation that he had had. He had told Henry that if he got the blood test, Willy would leave him alone, would start looking elsewhere for the real killer. The elsewhere that Pete was now convinced Willy would be looking was to "Carlisle," the Carlisle who was really Bentley, the Bentley whom Henry loved, whom Henry probably knew to be Bentley, and he was hiding from the blood test so that Willy would keep looking for *him,* so that the manhunt would indeed be put into effect for Henry, and they would therefore have to leave Bentley alone.

"I have to find him," said Connie.

"I'll go with you," said Pete, as simply and as naturally as he would have taken his next breath. Pete and Connie looked at each other, and quickly away.

They found Rita standing in the open doorway staring at the far turn in the road. "She's not on the late bus either," she said. "I told her to be on that bus *without fail.* I told her the White Mountains were *out* unless she unloaded her little fanny every single day this week from that bus and sat down in that room and did math. She's gone from a—"

"I think I know where she went," Connie interrupted her, as one would who had had long experience with Rita's harangues about Maxine. "I saw her going into the woods behind the school at the end of the day."

"The *woods?* The school *woods?* What in the world would she be doing in the school *woods?* There's nothing in there except about twenty tons of bull briars and poison ivy and—"

"The caves," said Pete, thinking not of Maxine but of Henry, and of Carlisle, and he and Connie looked at each other again, and this time neither was quite so quick to look away.

"The *caves!* Well, for heaven's sake, Pete! She's not going to go traipsing all the way through those woods to the *caves!* It's the end of September! It's not swimming weather! And besides, ever since Natalie Price got caught by the tide, I've told her the caves are off limits to her. It's dangerous out there, and there isn't one single solitary—"

"Travis Dearborn went that way. I think she—"

"You're right," said Pete in haste, riding over Connie and addressing Rita. "Of course she wouldn't have gone as far as the caves. Connie and I are going over to the school now to speak with Henry, and I'm sure she'll be around there somewhere. We'll bring her back with us if we see her." If they saw her. Pete had no idea where Maxine might be, but he was suddenly very sure that if he was right, and Henry was hiding, the caves were just exactly the kind of place Henry would be.

"I'll go with you," said Rita.

"No." Pete cleared his throat. "I mean, what if Maxine calls here? I think it would be better if one of us stayed by the phone." Now Rita was looking back and forth between Pete and Connie, and Pete could tell that she was beginning to latch on to something out of the ordinary, and the only thing that kept her from speaking was an inability to decide just what it was that she wanted to ask first. Pete decided to take advantage of the opportunity and edged out the door toward the truck.

Afterward, it seemed to Pete that a lot of what happened later could have been foreseen way back there when they first got into his truck. The minute Connie climbed up inside the cab beside him, something seemed to happen to her and she began to fuss around with the various impediments to comfort that Pete had allowed to accumulate on the seat of his second home. She picked up a coat hanger, glared at it, and tossed it onto the floor. She recovered the passenger side visor from the floor and for several seconds attempted to reattach it above the window before tossing it back down. She seemed to take an unnecessarily long time to pick a few potato chip crumbs from the seat belt before fastening it around her, and she used a slip from the dry cleaners to scrub at a circle of coffee that had spilled on the dash. It obliterated the cleaning slip but did nothing for the dash; Pete began to feel irritated. Many years ago the first thing that had made Pete suspect Connie had her priorities lined up in the right kind of row was the way she had thrown her clothes on the bedroom floor without a backward glance. Why was she flapping around with his stuff? Why was she opening up the crumbled dry-cleaning slip and trying to read it, for God's sake?

"A *suit?*" she said. "Since when did you own a *suit?*"

"It's not a suit," said Pete. "It's the brown jacket and some corduroy pants; Rennie just called it a suit because it came out cheaper that way."

"I didn't know Rennie gave discounts." She made it sound like Rennie was streetwalking.

"I think," said Pete carefully, "that if Henry is indeed hiding out, he might very well be hiding out at the caves. There aren't too many good hiding places around here, and the caves would give him plenty of time before the—"

"He isn't *hiding.*"

Pete looked out the window on his side and concentrated

on the blurred spikes of gray and green as the scrub pines whizzed by. His irritation was creeping up very close to anger, the violent furiousness with which he was becoming more and more acquainted of late. "I think," he continued, "that Henry might be hiding because he thinks Willy is going to look for Carlisle if he gives up on him. I don't think he wants Willy to give up on him. I think he's afraid that Carlisle is in trouble and he's trying to protect her."

Connie snorted.

Pete gripped the steering wheel hard with his good hand and down-shifted, wincing as he jammed his injured hand against the gearshift knob. Connie looked sideways just in time to catch him grimacing, but she looked away quickly, snorting again, but less so.

"And what makes you think Carlisle is in trouble? Willy hasn't said one word about her in all this; it's Henry he's out to get."

*Out to get.* These weren't the words of an enamored person. Pete risked a look sideways and saw that Connie was facing straight ahead, the neat angles of her nose and cheek and chin held high in what he had always thought of as her "chin-up" pose, a pose that he knew meant she was not feeling up at all. And what was it that made him think "Carlisle" was in trouble? Why didn't he tell her? Why didn't he explain to her every last detail about this whole foolish thing and let someone else sort it all out along with him? Suddenly he realized with a great wrenching pang how much he missed talking with her.

"I think it was Carlisle who was killed," he said, and he didn't stop when in his peripheral vision he saw her head snap around to face him. He explained, step by carefully enunciated step, the thinking that had led him to this conclusion.

When he got to the end, he sighed and looked at her.

Connie's incredulous expression collapsed, and she burst out laughing.

# Chapter 18

From the moment Connie swung herself up into Pete's truck with that same old familiar motion, she knew she was headed for emotional thin ice. She pushed a newspaper, a pair of vise grips, an empty chip bag, a golden Delicious apple, and a battered copy of *Great Expectations* into the center between them, and smelled in the cab that smell that she now knew would always remind her of him: the smell of engine oil and salt air (or was it the potato chips?) and soap and skin and freshly washed clothes.

She had lost him. She had done this unforgivable thing, this thing for which she had no real explanation other than the fear of never changing, never moving, never being a person all her own ever again. She had left without explanation, without confrontation, and the worst of it was that she knew deep down that the man who sat so far away from her now would have forgiven her this unforgivable thing right then if she had allowed him to do so, and somehow it was that fact more than any other that had driven her across the causeway with Glen Newcomb in tow. To have him hate her, *that* she could have borne, could have forgiven *him* for . . . Suddenly Connie stopped fussing with the junk that was pressing in all around her and almost let out a bitter laugh. He hated her now. That was clear. And still he sat there going into his usual act, trying to be so goddamned polite, trying to pretend nothing was wrong, trying to pretend that his hand wasn't killing him, the hand that he had busted up by hitting someone for saying something off-color about Ree Brown . . .

Ree Brown. She had not expected her to be here at Factotum, should have expected her to be there but had not done so, and once she had thrust herself into the middle, she had been unable to get herself out, had been unable to look at them, had come very near to the hated tears and humiliation she was finding it more and more difficult to fight. Fortunately for her, Pete seemed to have assumed that her state was due to concern for Henry.

Henry. And just like that he was offering to help her, offering to find Henry. Why? Now Pete was driving along being so goddamned chatty and patronizing about Henry! And what was he saying? She must not have been listening clearly. Something about Carlisle. Ree's daughter. Ree. Suddenly just looking at that bandaged hand made Connie feel furious. But what was this? Connie whipped around and stared at him and began to listen closer to what he was trying to tell her, to the reasons that he was ticking off one by one. *Carlisle* had died? *Carlisle?* And Bentley was the one who did it? To assume her more popular sister's favored life, to assume the ever-lusted-after Travis Dearborn for herself? Yes, Pete had cooked up a good one, something that would revolve around murderous, uncontrolled passions, something that would put the innocent male at the mercy of the wicked woman, something that would unravel all the inexplicable twists and turns that everyone's hormones were taking them on. And what was this he was saying about Ree? Nothing. Pete began, stumbled, stopped, left the subject of Ree alone, and Connie leaned back against the lumpy and yet somehow comforting upholstery and laughed until she cried and then cried for its own sake alone, but only for a minute and in such a way that she was sure she still looked like she was laughing. When she stopped she dried her eyes with the sleeve of her sweater and coughed a few times and pulled herself up straighter in the seat.

"You've been watching *The Parent Trap* again, is that it?"

No answer.

"You always were completely baffled by those twins, weren't you, Pete? You were *fascinated* by them, don't get me wrong, but baffled also. You never could keep them straight. But I think you're falsely assuming that others must necessarily possess your own shortcomings. I think Willy—"

"He asked *Maxine*," said Pete stiffly. "When we were there on the beach. How did she know it was Bentley? And Maxine gave some foolishness about her colors having been done, and Willy wanted to know about the colors. He wanted to know more about the colors."

"Well, someone had to identify the body, for chrissake. And I'm sure there were medical rec—"

"Ree Brown identified the body. And the medical records are the same, I know they are. Ree said they had all the same diseases, and they even cut their teeth in the same order on the same day, and—"

"Are you trying to tell me that there wasn't one single solitary mole, one scar, one—"

Pete remained silent.

"So Ree identified the body. So if it's the wrong twin, Ree knows, is that what you're saying?" Connie hoped that her tone sounded no more nor less intense at that particular moment, but Pete looked out the window to the left just then, and Connie somehow doubted it.

"If she did know, if one of her daughters came home stating that she was Carlisle and then Ree found out that it couldn't be, had to be Bentley, wouldn't she be put in the difficult position of having to turn in her one remaining child, wouldn't she be forced into protecting that one remaining child so as not to have to lose them both?"

It almost sounded as if he were quoting. But quoting what, some book he'd read, Ree herself, his own well-rehearsed thoughts? Connie stared at his profile, which was facing front again, and saw the strain and the pallor and thought that he was hurt much more than he was letting on, physically and perhaps emotionally as well. Was this what she had done to him? He sounded . . . not quite balanced somehow, lacking that inner surety that had once held him on an, at times, frighteningly even keel, and had set her off askew just by comparison, had made her always feel it was *her* fault, *her* problem, *her* improper thinking or feeling that somehow didn't jibe.

Pete pulled the truck up in the middle of the semicircular drive in the front of the aging bricks of the school steps, a spot where the students and the public were never allowed to park, and she could tell that he was parking there with an adolescent defiance that was also new to his nature. He got out of the truck, and when Connie did the same and stood beside him on the sidewalk, she shivered, but not from the nip in the air. But Pete looked her up and down coldly, moved to the back of the pickup, pulled out an old leather jacket, and tossed it to her over the truck bed. "We'll head straight for the caves," he said, "but we'll take the route you saw Maxine use, and look for her along the way."

She had been wrong. That moment of uncertainty seemed to have left him. He slammed the door to the truck and strode ahead of her along the walk that led from the main entrance around the building to the back. Was he angry with her for laughing at him? Connie almost laughed again. It would be just like him, with all those old reasons for anger still left unaddressed, to build himself into a rage over something new, something minor, something that had nothing at all to do with either of them. At least, thought Connie, she didn't think it did.

# Chapter
# 19

Maxine Peck charged into the bull briars without a thought for the fifty-six-dollar purple angora sweater that tugged at her shoulders and arms with every snag. Friday, she had said. Between the buses, she had said, a place where she would still be standing, alone, if she hadn't happened to look out the window just in time to see him disappearing in front of her very eyes into these very bull briars not a half hour ago. Maxine didn't like these woods, and she had been just as glad when her mother had put them off bounds to her with every threat that had ever meant anything to Maxine, threats that would translate well to her friends also, when she declined to go with them. But this was something else again. She was already in trouble for not coming home on the bus. She might as well go all the way and be in trouble for real since the White Mountains were out now anyway. Maxine stumbled over a stone, grabbed on to a branch, and fell down, scraping her palm on the branch bark as she went. She decided to stay sitting and collect herself. She pulled her offending foot up under her, sat back on her heels, and looked around.

The woods were thick with undergrowth, but it was late September and had been cold for some weeks as was the way with the weather on Nashtoba, and some of the leaves on the bushes had begun to shake loose. Or was it that they had been ripped loose by the trampling of feet before her? The path before her was almost like the deer tracks she and Pete used to find when she was little. She was getting the same feeling, the feeling of something having passed this way before them, something that had flattened the grass and bent back the branches and left a faint shadow of itself behind, something that would be waiting ahead if they were calm enough and quiet enough and didn't think scary thoughts. That's what Pete used to say to her: "Don't think scary thoughts, then you won't scare the deer." It had been easier back then not to think scary thoughts. Now she had Travis to think about, and Bentley to think about, and what her mother was going to do to her to think about . . . Her mother. It was all her mother's fault. If her mother would just stop *asking* her things every time she came home, she'd come home a lot more—as if she could explain any of those things anyway, like how her evening had been. As if, if she told her mother she had seen Travis, her mother wouldn't wreck it all by making That Face . . . *That Travis!*

Maxine got up and shook her head, enjoying the feeling of her hair clean and loose, remembering the searing jealousy when she overheard Travis commenting on the softness of Natalie's that day she leaned over his desk. She pushed that thought aside, along with the thought that Travis had not kept his promise about between the buses, and peered through the underbrush ahead of her, straining her ears for any sound.

Somehow it didn't surprise her that the sound she heard was that of someone crying.

# Chapter
# 20

Pete didn't give Connie a chance to pull up even with him. He used his extra height to its best advantage and stretched out his stride so that she had to take a hop every third step to keep up. Oh, he was furious with her! Laughing! It was the wrong twin, he knew it was, and *he* would be laughing when he had shown her, shown Willy, what was really going on. He careened around the corner of his old school building and almost collided into a girl coming out the side door, pausing to look at her just long enough to determine that it wasn't Maxine. It definitely wasn't. Whoever this girl was, she seemed to think that her main goal in life was to project every part of her body in his direction all at once, and the tortuous, sinuous result was almost worth laughing about if it weren't that Pete could still remember the day when that kind of thing would have at least slowed him in his tracks. It didn't today, not even when he heard Connie behind him saying, "Hello, Natalie," and heard the girl respond in a throaty whisper that also seemed to be directed at Pete, "Well, hello!"

"Jesus," Connie muttered behind him, once they rounded the last corner to the back of the building and were out of earshot. In front of them was the teachers' parking lot, and Pete could judge the lateness of the hour by the fact that there was only one car left in the lot, a not new red Trans Am.

"So where'd you see Maxine go?" he asked Connie, not turning to face her.

She didn't answer him. She circled past him and led on toward the woods, and despite himself, Pete felt something in the middle of him lurch at the old familiar sight of her in his beat-up leather jacket. She plunged ahead of him into the brush, and Pete had just time to think how insane this all was before he got smacked in the cheek with the first of the briars that Connie had whipped back up front.

"Watch it!" he hollered.

"Sor-*ree*," she snapped back, and Pete found he was starting to feel like *he* was fifteen, and not for the first time, of late.

# Chapter
21

Maxine pushed ahead toward the sound of the sobbing, and the first thing she recognized was the gold of Carlisle's jacket through the trees. The second thing she recognized was her voice.

"This is *it!* It's over!" Carlisle cried, and the tense and urgent voice of Travis Dearborn answered her.

"Please, Carlisle."

Maxine stayed still, hunkered down behind a young wild cherry and a tiny scrub pine that were so enmeshed with woodbine and briars as to make an almost solid screen.

"No, Travis. Not anymore."

"You know what this will do to me."

"No, I don't, and neither do you. And you had no business following me here."

"Why'd you come out here? Henry's out here, isn't he? It's because of Henry, isn't it?"

"No!"

All of a sudden Travis's voice altered in such a way that Maxine drew back.

"You lie. It *is* Henry. You came here after Henry, didn't you? He didn't show up today. He had the big blood test today. It *was* him, wasn't it? He ran out here and you followed him."

Still Carlisle didn't speak. Maxine peered around the vines, but she couldn't see Carlisle at all anymore. Then Travis stooped down and yanked her to her feet from somewhere down below, as if she had wilted.

"No!" She pulled away from Travis and turned and ran, crashing through the woods not unlike a frightened deer. Travis remained standing there, looking at his empty hands, as if still seeing who had been in them and was now gone.

So Travis and Carlisle were through. It was as Maxine had heard in school, but had not dared to believe.

She crept out from her screen of leaves and vines and walked up behind Travis.

He whipped around. "Oh *God,*" he said, "Not *you* . . ."

# Chapter
# 22

All of a sudden Connie stopped dead in her tracks, and Pete, engrossed in his own reminiscences behind her, didn't slow down soon enough and had to push past her to avoid crashing into her.

"I heard something."

"A deer." Don't think scary thoughts, Pete recited to himself.

"Deer, my ass," said Connie. "Someone's running like hell. Over there." She appeared to listen for another minute. "And crying."

Swell. Pete, listening, could hear it too. He moved off in the direction of the sound.

"Hey!" Connie reached from behind and caught his jacket. "I think we better leave whoever it is alone."

"It might be Maxine."

"So what? You think she wants to cry on your shoulder?"

"She might be hurt."

"Hurt! She's running like an elephant! *Into* the woods, not out."

"Maybe somebody's after her."

"Bentley Brown, no doubt?"

Pete ripped his jacket from Connie's grip, broke into a jog, and began to tear through the woods. *Bentley Brown, no doubt!* He wanted to kill her. He wanted to throw her over a cliff. *He wanted to make her pay.* He pulled out a fistful of bull briar by the roots, kicked a dead limb off a tree, smashed through a thicket of poison ivy, and stopped dead in his tracks.

It *was* Bentley. She was sprawled out on the other side of a tenacious vine that was stretched taut under her shin; she was still crying, tugging at her leg to free it. As Pete came charging through the woods in a spray of bark and briars, she looked up, her gold jacket and navy pants torn and muddied. Pete stopped where he stood and said her name. "Bentley?"

It was an eerie thing to see fear come to her face and to know that he had caused it. At first she just looked puzzled to see him there, her eyes absorbing a piece of information that her brain could not process, but as soon as he spoke her name, her pupils seemed to dilate and then contract, her trapped body shrinking away from him with a response that was as old as the hills. Fight or flight, fight or flight, fight or flight, he could almost see her adrenal glands screaming it out along taut nerves. She gave one final vicious yank with her leg, broke free, got up, and ran.

Pete stood there, momentarily frozen by the novel experience of having someone afraid of him, someone running away from him, and in that moment of stopped time Connie puffed up behind him and again grabbed him by the jacket. "Have you lost your mind?"

Pete pulled himself free of her and continued in the direction in which Bentley had run, calling her name again, but by now there was no sight of her, and no sound.

*"Bentley,"* Connie repeated, this time looking at him with extreme disbelief. "You have," she said finally. "You have lost your mind!"

# Chapter
# 23

Maxine stood in front of Travis and blinked. Behind him she could see the lightness in the sky that signified the end of woods, the beginning of the cliffs and caves at the edge of the sea. She looked out to where she imagined the sea would be and said, "You were supposed to meet me."

"Meet you! What do you think I'm doing, wandering around out here for my health? Something came up. So we've met. So what is it? Come on."

Maxine raised her chin up high. "You'd better be nice to me, that's what I came to tell you!" It wasn't, of course, what she had come to tell him at all, but suddenly things seem to come into focus once more for Travis, and he moved in closer to her, forcing Maxine, suddenly nervous, to back away.

Travis held up his hands. "I'd better be nice to you. Why?"

"I saw you!" she burst out. "I saw you in the gym! I watched you! I always stay and watch you, I saw you with the screwdriver, I heard you banging at the lockers, I know you did it, I know you took the ring!" Maxine, having said it now, having come out with the thing that had weighed so heavily on her mind, looked at Travis with horror, and listened to her own words now pounding around in the air.

He was silent and still. And then he sprang toward her, and Maxine jumped back.

"You saw nothing! What are you talking about? You didn't see anything! I didn't have any screwdriver!"

He kept coming toward her, and Maxine kept edging backward until she stumbled. She turned, moved into a clearer space, and continued to edge back, trying to explain, to set it right, to have him understand.

"It's okay, Travis. I know you can explain it, I didn't mean I was going to tell anybody, I've known all along and I haven't told anyone! Not anyone! I *won't* tell, either. I won't because of something else I have to tell you, what I really wanted to tell you, what I would have told you first if you weren't being so rotten. I love you, Travis."

"Aagh!" He lunged toward her, but something in his face made the move less than affectionate, and Maxine instinctively backed away. She was almost on the shale of the cliffs now, just above the caves, and as she backed up, she stumbled, suddenly feeling dizzy as if her feet were letting go of her, as if the earth were floating away below her. It was! She was in space, falling through a hole that had opened in the earth and swallowed her, and although she felt nothing at first, she knew she was hitting things as she fell. Then she landed.

She was lying on the rocks and sand at the bottom of one of the caves. She tried to push herself up with her arms and found that one arm wouldn't work right, and as she tried to get her feet under her, hot fire shot through her body from one of her legs. She looked down. She could see through the tight jeans that her upper leg had an alarming jog in it, and when she moved her leg to get a better look at it, she felt a pain like nothing she had ever felt before, pain that made her sick to her stomach. Her head and shoulder throbbed. She looked around. The cave she was lying in was not like the others she had seen along the shore. This cave was solid on all sides except for what looked like a narrow tunnel at its base and, of course, the hole in its roof through which she had fallen. She flipped onto her back and looked out of the dark hollow in which she lay at the circle of sky that seemed miles above her.

Travis Dearborn peered down over the edge. She closed her eyes and moaned. Thank God. She felt dizzy, unreal, nauseated. She heard a whooshing sound in her ears and then it was over her and in her mouth and eyes, a cold, freezing wave of water that sloshed through that narrow tunnel and into the cave where she lay and seeped back out again before she had quite realized it had come. Then another one! She struggled up onto her elbows to keep her face above the water, and when the third wave hit, it left an inch of water under her. She looked up, and high on the walls of the cave, far above her head, she could see the mark that the last rising tide had left. At least six more feet above that was the hole in the sky that framed Travis Dearborn. Travis looked back down, first at her, and then at the tunnel where the water roared in and sucked back out, leaving a little more of itself each time.

He backed slowly away from the hole, less and less of his torso visible, until she could see only his eyes and the top of his head.

"Travis!"

He blinked once.

"Travis!" she screamed, but he was gone.

# Chapter
24

It took Maxine a long time to latch on to some pretty simple facts. The first was that the pain she was having was no worse than she should have expected after having fallen over fifteen feet onto rocks. She was able to narrow her general rotten condition into four major trouble spots—her wrist, her shoulder, her leg, and her head. She was sure her swollen wrist was at least sprained if not broken, her shoulder was possibly dislocated, and her leg was definitely fractured up where it angled sickeningly and gave her such grating pain. She didn't know what was wrong with her head other than that it ached at the back and she was very dizzy. She wondered as she watched the water whether she was completely *with it* all the time—didn't it seem that if she closed her eyes for one second, when she opened them another whole foot of water had crept into the cave?

And that was the second fact, that the cave in which she was lying was slowly, or not slowly, depending on her present state of consciousness, filling up with water which continued to crash in through the narrow tunnel at the bottom of the cave. She had thought, at first, that she was just disoriented, that the sand and the water and the sky and the rocks were all around her on one level and it was only her head that was spinning, creating the ebb and flow, that once she settled down and found a stick of some sort to lean on, she would be able to set off on her hike back home.

It was odd, she thought, that the third fact, the fact that the only ways out of this cave were a tunnel that was too narrow and a hole at the top of a shaft that was too high, hadn't occurred to her first, before the pain and the water, but it hadn't. Only after she saw the water, figured out about the water, did she look around and realize that she was way down inside the earth, that around her were rocky walls with the only ledge on which she could perch too far up for her to reach, that it would have been very hard if not impossible to get out of this hole if she were uninjured, and that injured, she didn't have a prayer.

The fourth fact, the most painful one and the most serious, at least to Maxine, was the fact that Travis Dearborn had seen her fall, had been partly responsible for her falling, had looked over the edge into the cave and had seen the tunnel and the water, and had left her there and was not coming back.

It had never *really* occurred to Maxine that Travis had hurt Bentley, that it could have been Travis who was wanted by the police, but still, she suspected about the ring, suspected that he had broken open the gym locker and stolen Henry's ring, and therefore must have lost his *somewhere,* though not necessarily at the beach. Even as she began to shiver in the last-day-of-September air, even as she tried to prop herself against the wall of the cave with her head above the wash of the tide, she didn't quite believe that he had spoken to her the way he had, that he had left, really left, not planning to return at all. Her imagined world, the world she and Travis had traveled around in together so often in her mind, seemed equally as real as the present one, and she looked up quite often, expecting to see him, thinking that she really did see him once or twice. A final whoosh of water smashed into the cave from the tunnel and knocked her down and under. She came up coughing and gasping, unable to regain a purchase, shivering for real every time a part of her now-soaked body was able to rise up out of the water and into the cold air. But then the water stopped whooshing. The tide, she knew, as did every Nashtoba child, would now rise quietly, calmly, steadily, until it reached its high-water mark. She looked again at the line on the wall of the cave that had been left by the last high tide. It was well over her head, but far below the opening to the sky. She knew that she could struggle to keep afloat until she was too cold and hurting and tired to do so, and then . . .

The fourth fact, the fact that Travis Dearborn wasn't coming back, sank in just a second before the fifth one, that she was going to die in this stinking rotten place, and with that realization came the suddenly terrifyingly clear sixth one—that Travis Dearborn had murdered Bentley Brown, and Maxine was the only one who really knew it, that he would leave her there to die so then *no one* would know it, and he would be safe.

Maxine tried to let herself be buoyed by the water, to use it instead of fighting against it. It seemed to help. Even the pain in her leg seemed to ease momentarily. She wasn't aware of a great deal of time passing, but suddenly she noticed that the ledge that had seemed so elusive before was now closer, that she could hook her good arm over the lowest end and, with a good deal of pain that seemed to do funny things to her sense of time, pull herself up.

She clung to the ledge with desperate fingers, knowing that if she let go, she'd die, just as Travis wanted, just as he was counting on. First Bentley, then Maxine.

But suddenly, as Maxine thought about Travis and about how much she had loved him and how little he had cared in return, the fact that she might die didn't seem to matter to her anymore. Somehow her fingers seemed to sense at once that if they gave up their shaky hold on the ledge, it would be okay, it wouldn't matter. A halfhearted debate set in between her fingers and her brain, but she knew that she was only a bystander to it, that as she lay there and watched and listened to the arguments, she could, by doing nothing, let her adrenaline seep away.

# Chapter
25

Connie was beginning to feel a little afraid of him, a little afraid of this Pete she didn't know who ripped through the woods one-handed on the trail of some poor crying girl who he decided had killed her sister and then taken her place. This fearfulness was slowing her down, turning her thoughtful, giving her pause all of a sudden. What had happened to him? The man she used to know so well would have been the last to suspect this full gamut of treachery and lies, would never have believed a seventeen-year-old girl capable of cold-blooded killing, let alone plotting the deceit that would have had to follow. He would never have believed someone like Henry would contribute to such a lie, or that someone like Ree, who was herself personally involved with him, would use the relationship to . . .

Treachery and lies. And suddenly Connie could see how all this had very much to do with both of them, how Pete would now be quick to believe the worst in people because he had seen it all firsthand in her, how this anger that she felt in him was toward her and her alone, but instead of putting it where he wanted to put it, he was spreading it out all over the lot. He was frightening her right now, and still she followed along behind, more afraid to leave him than she was to stay with him. It was going to have to be up to her to talk sensibly to him, to make him see that Bentley was *dead,* to keep her own cool for once in her life.

A bull briar snapped through the air and yanked a tuft of hair out of her scalp. "Ow! Jesus, watch it, will ya?"

Pete turned around and glared at her.

"Wait a minute!"

Pete continued to charge through the forest, and Connie's full five seconds of patience had worn out. *"Wait one minute,* I said!"

*"What!"*

He stopped. She had his full attention, his full hatred. So fine. It was what she had wanted, after all, some real feeling directed at its real target, and now if she could only stop having this idiotic desire to *cry* all the time . . . "We're looking for Henry, not Bentley." Oh, a flash of triumph in his eyes when she said that name Bentley! "Or whoever she is. We're supposed to be looking at the caves, we're not supposed to be chasing people into poison ivy. And the caves are this way." She pointed behind her, and then despite herself, her arm slid around a little, first to the right, and then to the left. She wasn't so sure all of a sudden from just which direction they had come.

"The caves are this way," said Pete, pointing in front, and without further discussion, he resumed his march. Oh, she could hate him too, she knew it now! Mr. Perfect, Mr. Right, Mr. Daniel Boone! The woods, his life, her life, everything all mapped out and waiting, waiting only for him to put one foot in front of the other and follow along the path! She tripped along behind him, not because she was afraid of him now or afraid for him but because she was afraid for herself and where she was, not only in these woods but in the general scheme of things. She turned around to pull her arm free of a briar, and when she looked to the front again, she couldn't see him. For a second she felt a chill of panic until he rose from where he had been squatting just off to the right of the path.

"Well, Tonto?" He ignored her, the meticulous straightness of his back the only clue that he had heard her at all. So his sense of humor was gone too. Connie laughed out loud.

"Shut up, I'm trying to listen."

Shut up? Shut *up!* "I *would* shut up," said Connie, "I really would shut up, the only trouble is—"

*"Shut up."*

She did, more out of shock than anything, and as soon as she did, she heard what he must have been hearing all along—it wasn't crying, it wasn't even definitely human, but it was a noise that somehow didn't sound right, didn't sound like the kind of thing it would be okay to ignore. Pete looked over his shoulder at her as if to make sure she was there, and then he began to run again, as fast as he could move through the suddenly thinning brush, the sky in some strange way growing lighter now even as it got closer to evening. Connie pressed on after him, her eyes glued to him, watching him stumble and catch himself and hold himself stiff in a moment of what she knew must be pain. She shut her mind to him, shut her mind to the noise, refusing to think of anything but keeping up with him as they ran. Once, no, twice more he looked behind him, and seeing her there, his eyes showing nothing but indifference now, he pushed on faster. When he broke through the edge of the trees and into the bayberry and beach plum that lined the rocks that marked the start of the cliffs, he stopped and listened again. This time it sounded human. It sounded like human *coughing*. It sounded like a human coughing into a trash barrel, one that was lying in the very bottom of a landfill full of rain. Pete and Connie looked at each other, and then crept forward side by side over the underbrush. The sound grew louder, stopped, then started again, and echoed out of the very ground below their feet. Then all of a sudden there was no ground, nothing but the raw edges of a hole, and Connie looked down into the cave and saw Maxine.

She was clinging to a thin shelf of rock projecting from one side of the cave wall. The bottom of the cave was full of water, and the coughing sound was Maxine, as she tried to get the water she had already swallowed out of her lungs. Maxine had managed to pull herself onto the ledge, one hand hooked over the high end, one knee buckled under her where she half lay on it. Something seemed to be wrong with the other arm and the other leg. Connie felt her stomach turn over—the upper part of Maxine's leg looked like a bent spoon. Neither Pete nor Connie spoke. Maxine didn't look up, but all of a sudden it seemed to Connie that she deliberately straightened out that one crucial hand, and she slid off the ledge and into the water.

"Maxine!" Pete hollered, and Connie could feel him gather himself beside her. She reached out and grabbed his arm as hard as she could, but he flipped out of her grasp and over the side of the hole, yelping as his bad hand and his bad side took his weight. He lost his grip and fell. He disappeared into, and under, the water. He was gone.

"Pete!" Connie rolled onto her belly, slid over the edge of the hole, dangled for one long second, and let go. She hit the water hard, and it was forced up her nostrils as she went under, then she was back up spluttering and splashing and lashing out with her feet until she could feel a smooth space to stand up on. The water was waist-high, and Pete was back up on its surface now also. He looked at Maxine, and then he looked up at the hole fifteen feet above them, and then he looked at Connie, and she had never in all her life seen him so angry.

# Chapter
## 26

It had come as a surprise to Pete, the intense pain in his
injured hand and side as he hung from the edge of the hole,
pain that only doubled with the sudden impact with the
water. He let himself sink down through the water while
he grappled with the pain, then scrambled against the rocky
bottom for a foothold so that he pushed up to the surface
when he was just about out of air and WHAM! A second
explosion of water came with a blow that pushed him under
again, and when he finally broke the surface, gasping, he
couldn't believe his eyes. *Connie.* She was in the cave
along with him, looking like she'd seen a ghost, splashing
around like she was drowning in a mix of leather and water.
Pete reached out and yanked at his leather jacket, steadying
her on her feet, then he sloshed across the cave, scooped
Maxine up in his arms, and propped her on the ledge, holding her away from him only long enough to look her over.

Her face was white and her lips blue, her eyes oddly
unfocused, her jet black hair plastered to her scalp, making
her head seem small and lumpy. He looked at her arm and
her leg and looked away quickly. "Are you all right?" he
asked, and even though she was so very obviously not all
right, she nodded.

She began to cry, seeming at the moment to want most

of all to lean there pitched into his chest where he could hold her, so he didn't move her, but stared over her head at Connie.

"What exactly," he said to her, making a very good effort at keeping his voice calm for Maxine's benefit, "did you hope to achieve by that particular little—"

"God*damn* it, what is the matter with you?" Connie hollered at him, and floundered across the pool, fluttering her hands over Maxine and Pete without actually touching either of them. "Jesus *Christ,* you need your head examined! Mr. Macho! Sure, I have only one arm and half a brain, but I can do it! I can save us all! I can climb tall buildings with a—"

"And this is your big solution?" Pete hissed. "To jump into the cave on top of me? Have you ever in your entire life once thought beyond the present moment? Has it occurred to you that with all three of us in here, it leaves no one else who's out? Did that occur to you? Did it?"

She stopped squawking at him. She looked up above them at the circle of sky and blinked her eyes. The gold clip had come out of her hair somewhere along the route, her hair was dripping into her face, his leather jacket hung from around her neck like something dead and rotten, and she looked so miserable that Pete turned to Maxine almost with relief.

The lumpiness of Maxine's head was more than just mere lumpiness—a large egg was jutting out from the right-hand side of the back of her skull. She no longer seemed to be crying. Her eyes were closed, and with her one good arm she clung to the collar of his denim jacket, the arm with the damaged wrist hanging limp at her side. Connie seemed to have noticed the lump too. She reached out and touched it, and Maxine winced and opened her eyes.

"Good. She's not out, but she still might have a concussion. And she should probably keep that arm up, not down."

Pete said nothing to Connie, but helped Maxine to settle more comfortably on the ledge and, as he did so, asked a series of what he thought were very meticulous questions about her injuries. When he got through, Connie aggravated him further by asking about twenty more, by repositioning the deformed leg, and then by struggling out of the wet leather jacket in order to use it to cover Maxine.

Pete whipped off his own soaking jacket, wincing only once as the shoulder movement activated the burning in his side, and tried to remember what he had learned about wet and cold. Wool and some synthetics, he knew, maintained warmth even if wet, but cotton did not. He didn't know about leather. But even if his own jacket wasn't warm, it would keep the wind that was circling down and around them from reaching Maxine. Wind, he knew, was very cold. He shivered, pulled the leather jacket up higher onto Maxine's shoulders, and spread his denim one over her legs.

Connie splashed across the cave, and Pete turned to find her examining the side of the cave with her hands.

"So let's see you single-bound your way out of this one," she said.

"I wouldn't have to single-bound my way out of anything if you hadn't—"

"You didn't tell me you were going to go scuba diving while you were down there, all right? I thought you hit something and got knocked out, all right? I made a mistake, all right?" She looked at Maxine, stopped hollering, and slipped and slid her way back across the cave.

"I think she's out, but she's breathing okay. It's probably best to leave her. I don't see why we should wake her up, just so she can suffer along with us." She shivered. Pete looked up along the walls of the cave toward the hole of light that was getting dimmer by the minute above them.

"There are people around, I bet," said Connie. "Henry, for instance. And Carlisle."

Pete snapped around, wanting to say something about its being Bentley who was around, but Connie went right on.

"I mean we could start hollering or something."

Pete didn't feel like hollering. He splashed along one

wall, looking at its smooth surface, straining his eyes for hand- and toeholds, and as if she could read his mind, Connie said, "If you think for one minute you're going to climb up that with your bad hand, you're nuts! Give me a boost!"

She was right, of course. The purchase was lousy, if it even existed, and his hand was also lousy. It looked like there might be a place to jam a toe a few feet up on the side across from Maxine's little ledge, and who knew what was up there after that? As the walls narrowed toward the surface, Connie might be able to swing herself out and boost herself enough to grab the edge of the hole where the roots and rock ledge were exposed, but she could never pull herself up and over. And what if she crashed into the sides on the way down, landed wrong . . . ?

"Let me try," said Pete, and he lifted his own foot in preparation.

Connie stared at him.

"Come on, it's getting dark."

Connie braced herself in the water, really shivering all over now, Pete noticed, and laced her fingers together to give him a stirrup in which to start. He put his foot in her hands. He gave a half bounce, then a full bounce, then launched himself up against the stone wall and groped for the projecting rock with his free foot while raking the wall for a good grip with his good hand. The searing pain in his side as he elevated his arm lasted only as long as it took him to transfer the other arm high, clutch at the slimy wall with his bad hand, find a protrusion, and realize that he was incapable of gripping it. Everything seemed to give way at once—hand, foot, other hand, other foot—and he crashed and slid over stone and into water for a second time that day. On the ledge where Connie held her, Maxine moaned and stirred, and Pete half sloshed, half swam toward her, but she didn't make any more noise.

Neither did Connie. At least not for a half a second or two. *"Swell! Terrific! Now* what did you hurt?"

"Nothing," Pete snapped back at her.

"Then will you give me a boost and just shut up about it, please?"

Pete righted himself, braced himself, began to make a stirrup with one swollen, frayed, and bandaged hand and one that was now scraped and bleeding, and thought better of the plan. "Here," he said. "Let's go shoulders instead." He ducked down into the water, and Connie, catching on at once to an old game they used to play, scrambled up onto his shoulders, holding on to his hands first, then his head, then the wall, as he raised himself slowly and propelled her toward the holds that had not worked for him. As Pete steadied her on his shoulders, Connie steadied herself against the wall, and up they rose. She stretched up, and it almost seemed to be enough, to be within reach, to be the answer, but no. The hole in the sky still loomed several feet beyond Connie's reach.

"Boost me up!"

Pete clutched her ankles harder. "No."

"I said boost me up!"

"No."

"If you don't boost me up there, I'm going to kill you when I get down! I can make it! Just shoot me up there! I can pull myself over—"

"No you can't."

"No I can't! You'd rather die in this hole than—"

Pete applied pressure to Connie's ankles, angling her to the fore, causing her finally to slide off his shoulders and down his chest, his arms slowly lowering her. She twisted herself around, trying to wrench out of his grip before her feet were under her, sliding and lurching around on the uneven underwater floor, desperate to get away from him.

"Let me go! Don't touch me! I don't want you—"

"I think you've made that perfectly clear on several occasions," said Pete, and he let her go. She slithered under the water, but when she came up, she came up spouting.

"Oh, you think so! A lot you know about it! And what about you? You wouldn't ever say what you really felt, would you, how you *hate* me, have hated me ever since I left with Glen!''

Pete winced and felt the pain of the wince, as well as of the words, still, after all this time, as if he were just hearing them for the first time. And really, wasn't he? Wasn't this the first time that that dreaded name had come up between them?

From what now seemed like a long distance away, Connie, wet and white and shaking, continued in a tearing, throbbing voice that seemed to ring around the cave and out the top of it for all the world to hear. "Oh, that's right, Pete. Don't say anything. Don't admit how angry you are because I left you with another man. Pretend it didn't hurt, you never cared, you never minded, and then blame me for something else, for jumping into the cave, for trying to help Maxine, for laughing about Bentley, for trusting Henry . . .''

Pete could say nothing, couldn't speak, couldn't look at her anymore, couldn't listen. He turned and worked his way through the now chest-high water to check on Maxine. The water was rising fast, but he could see the lines the tide had left on the wall and knew it would stop there sooner or later. The lines were too high. Or too low. The tide wouldn't stop until it was above all their heads, but it was going to stop far from the hole above them, and Pete took some seconds to wonder how many minutes of treading water while battling cold and injuries the three of them would be able to withstand. He turned around and found Connie, eyes huge and aching in a dead-white face, watching him look up and down the walls of the cave.

"Pete," she said, and there was something different in her voice, something new, or was it something old? But before he could figure it out, he heard something else— from up above. He looked up, and there, peering over the edge of the hole, was Travis Dearborn.

# Chapter
27

It seemed to Maxine that ever since she was a little girl, Peter Bartholomew had been dropping out of the sky into her life at the very moment when she happened to be needing him most, like when her mother and father had gotten divorced, like when her mother was being a jerk, like when she was having those nightmares about Bentley, so she wasn't much surprised, not really, to find that just as she was about to die, he came dropping down on her once again, this time bringing Connie along with him.

Maxine had once been pretty mad at Connie, the same way she had been mad at her father once, but then Pete had explained that she shouldn't be mad at Connie either, and that was what seemed so strange right now. Pete was mad at Connie. Really mad at her. That very first minute when Pete looked at Maxine and held on to her, it seemed to her that he was almost afraid, and in that one minute she felt the most afraid she had ever felt in her whole life, but not two minutes later she realized that he wasn't afraid, he was just mad, mad at Connie, and then Maxine kind of went out of it and heard only dimly some angry words that flashed back and forth in her dreams.

It was a single word that snapped her back, a name, actually, and it rattled around in her aching, throbbing head

before it drove her eyes open and got her to sit up. Pete was saying the name, sounding glad, and something was wrong with that. She heard the name and looked up and saw the face that went with it looming over them at the edge of the hole. Travis. She screamed.

Pete was there, holding on to her again, trying to warm her up, telling her it was going to be all right, Travis was going to get help.

"No," said Maxine. "He won't. He won't." She struggled for the right words to explain it, to explain who Travis was and what he had done, and just then another head appeared above them, the head of Carlisle Brown. Travis didn't see her. As he crouched over the hole, peering into it, staring at Maxine, straining to hear what she was trying to say, Carlisle's arms swung high over her head, a huge rock in her hand. She was going to kill Travis. She was going to save them.

"Look out! Bentley!" Pete hollered, and Travis responded to the warning with a turn and a sweep of his athlete's arm that brought Carlisle's rock to the ground.

Another voice. Another voice from up there somewhere, but too far away for Maxine to be able to tell who it was, and Travis whipped around in response to it, giving Carlisle a chance to run. The sounds of feet echoed into the cave through the earth, through the shale and roots—what must have been Carlisle's feet with Travis's after her, running away from the cave.

# Chapter
# 28

Connie stared from Pete to Maxine and from Maxine to Pete, trying to decide which of them looked worse. Pete's face had closed in on itself and aged ten years the very minute she had said the name "Glen," and Maxine, for some reason, had started screaming and shaking the minute Travis's face appeared over the edge of the hole. And neither one of them was making any sense.

"Bentley," said Pete. "She was going to kill him. He knows."

"Travis," said Maxine. "He did it. He had a screwdriver."

"Henry will get help," said Connie, and despite the fact that Bentley was dead and Travis had had no screwdriver, both Pete and Maxine looked at *her* as if she were the crazy one, and said in unison, *"Henry?"*

"Yes, Henry. I think that was Henry who yelled. Carlisle will tell him we're in here and he'll go get some help and—"

"She isn't going to tell him a damned thing. She knows I know she's Bentley and she's going to take off like a shot, and Henry's going to go with her. I only hope Travis doesn't keep after them and forget about us."

"Travis!" said Connie, thrashing her arms to keep warm. Travis, the last person in the world Connie felt like count-

ing on for help, and here Pete was pinning all their hopes on him because he happened to look like Superman himself. And this Bentley business! But she wasn't going to go into Pete's asinine twin theory all over again in front of Maxine. Maybe Maxine hadn't noticed that he had yelled out Bentley's name. Maybe she wasn't listening. She looked only half-there, and the things she seemed bent on saying weren't coming out too straight, but she didn't seem to be shivering anymore. Pete was carefully rubbing her uninjured arm and back to keep her warm.

"It was Travis," Maxine said over and over again. "Travis. He was fighting with Carlisle. She ran away. I told him everything. He scared me, he came after me, I ran and fell, and he left me."

Pete didn't seem to be listening to her. He was staring at Connie. "And what makes you so sure that was Henry?" he asked, his voice colder than she was.

"I heard him. He'll be back."

"You heard him. He'll be back. I suppose that's why he was running the other way?"

"He was *not* . . ." she began, but Pete snorted.

"Okay," said Connie, forgetting in her second wave of fury her earlier concerns about Maxine. "Let's have it. Bentley Brown killed her sister. Took her place. Henry knows and is helping her, that's why he's here instead of taking a blood test; he wants Willy to keep chasing after *him* instead of her. Ree Brown knows, of course, but is protecting her daughter also, using you in the process to . . . to what?"

"To keep in touch with Willy. Keep her informed of what *he* knows and keep me distracted from what *I* know."

Connie stared at him. He was serious. "And Travis Dearborn? Being Carlisle's boyfriend, you assume he knows? So that's why Bentley was going to kill him just now?"

"He killed *her*," said Maxine, and this time Pete seemed to hear her, and this time Connie realized what exactly it was she was trying to say. Travis. Oh God, she knew it! The almighty Travis! But why???

"I *told* you. He stole Henry's ring. I saw him. I told him I saw him. He came after me and I fell in here. He left me to die."

Connie stared at Maxine, who was crying now in big, gulping sobs, and looked up from Maxine's stricken face where it pressed into Pete's chest to his equally stricken one. Connie knew at once by that face, and by the barely perceptible rubbing motion in Pete's one good hand as he tried to keep Maxine warm, that he was in more pain than before, more of that old double-edged kind of pain. *Now* what had happened? Something more than what she could take the blame for, something more than just her speaking the name "Glen" out loud. It was as if someone else had just let him down. But who? And by doing what?

# Chapter
# 29

No, thought Pete. Not Travis. It couldn't be Travis. He had watched him on the beach, had seen him strike Henry, had thought, yes, I know this boy, this almost-man, I know how he feels, I can see how violence comes to you when you least expect it, what anger does when you let it consume you, when you let it control you. But never, never had he thought his own anger, his own violence, his own blow against Jimmy Solene, which had seemed the same stuff of which Travis's had been made, could have gone further, could have led to more blows, could have led to . . . yes, could have led to murder. Travis murdered Carlisle. Of course, it was the final proof for Pete that the dead twin was indeed Carlisle. There was no reason in the world for Travis to have harmed Bentley, but Carlisle, yes. Jealousy. And Henry must have been the cause, was surely the cause, was now so clearly the father of Carlisle's child and the person who had driven Travis over the edge not once, but twice. Once to commit murder when Carlisle confessed to him? Yes. And twice when he saw the same man on the same beach with his arm around not the same girl but almost the same girl, doing the same thing again, starting all over again to steal the girl that he believed Travis loved. It had been pride, of course, that had sparked that one last blow, nothing but hurt pride.

But why would Bentley go along with this deception? Why would Bentley now assume her sister's place to protect her sister's boyfriend, the very boyfriend who had murdered her? Because *she* loved him. Because, as Pete had suspected all along, she had wanted to assume her more popular sister's life, had wanted this big prize, this Travis Dearborn that everyone loved and wanted. Look at Maxine! She had loved him. She had wanted to talk to Pete about this, had known all about this, had known Travis killed Carlisle and still wanted to protect him to the point that she wouldn't speak to Pete unless he promised to keep it from the police. And that's why she was sobbing so uncontrollably right now, not from pain or cold or fear, but because she had loved this person who had left her to die. Love. Love was more important than right and wrong, love was everything; hadn't Pete learned that above everything else by now? Connie had not loved him. No, to be fair, he had to say it wasn't quite as bad as that. She had once loved him, he could not deny that, could not accept a lie as gross as that. But she hadn't loved him enough, had *stopped* loving him. She had fallen in love with Glen Newcomb. She had left him for Glen without a thought for the right or the wrong or the hurt or the pain or the anger . . . And yes, Connie was right about that, too, the anger, although it had taken him a long time to admit that he felt it, longer still to track it to its source. Poor Jimmy Solene! Poor Travis. How far would Travis's anger take him? Would he really, truly, leave three more people here to die to protect what, in that first moment of anger, had cost him so much?

Pete's feet slipped from under him and he thrashed around, clinging to Maxine's ledge, regaining his foothold with effort. Connie was watching him, and there seemed to be something about her look that was different. She met his eye for a long minute. She struggled through the shoulder-deep water, pushed him away from Maxine and up against the side of the cave, setting to work herself to keep Maxine warm in his place.

"I *was* angry," said Pete. "I *am* angry."

"I know. I know. You had a right."

"You should have told me. You should have told me you loved him."

"Love! Love had nothing to do with it."

*Nothing to do with it??*

She sighed. "I can't explain it. I couldn't then."

"You should have tried."

"I did try!" Connie jerked around, and Maxine groaned in her arms. Pete pushed away from the wall, but Connie waved him back and resettled herself so that Maxine was supported more comfortably. "At least I wanted to. But I couldn't understand how I could feel so . . . so *strangled* and you be so happy. I figured it had to be me." Connie turned away. "One perfect man, one perfect life, the only thing that didn't fit was me, the imperfect woman. So I left. Poor Glen didn't know what hit him."

Perfect. Perfect? The word was like a wound. And suddenly Pete saw it all, or at least he saw some of it, his own doubts and insecurities masked by a veneer that piled up in layers as it had more doubts and insecurities to mask. She had not been happy, he could see that now, would have to admit in all honesty that he had seen it then, had not known how to deal with it other than to try to make things *seem* perfect, to keep from her his own fears, to hide his own unhappiness that grew inevitably with hers until he had buried it so deep that neither of them knew it was there.

But wait a minute! This wasn't *his* fault. *She* was in the wrong, and he was in the right, she had slept with Glen Newcomb, and then she had walked out! *Glen Newcomb.* Glen Newcomb, who supposedly didn't know what hit him? "He knew perfectly well what hit him," said Pete. *"I* was the one who didn't know what hit."

"I wanted to talk to you. I tried. But you weren't like

189

me. You were never afraid, or unsure, you didn't seem to need me. You loved your life—"

"I loved *you*," said Pete, and he watched Connie's face screw up, as if in physical pain, but still, it was not as great a pain as his own, and now the angry words wouldn't stop. "And I was afraid plenty! I was afraid after you left, I can tell you that! And I was afraid *before* you left. I was *never* perfect, I . . ." Oh God, what a joke this was. "I *loved* you," he said again.

"Loved," said Connie. *"Loved."*

"You *left* me."

"I left you." The words were dull and empty.

*I would have left with you,* he wanted to say. I loved you, he wanted to say again, but slowly Pete was beginning to suspect something else. Could it be true that love was *not* everything? He leaned against the wall, cold, exhausted, nearing the end of his emotional and physical rope, hearing the rumble and roll of all the words inside his head. He needed to get out of this cave before he could think any more about this. He needed to know that Maxine was safe and warm, that Connie was, that he was, before he could spare more effort on the dilemma of his marriage. But when a head appeared again at the edge of the hole against the sky, Pete was unable to decide if it represented their doom or their salvation. All he knew was that he didn't want the head to leave. It was time to get this settled, one way or the other.

"Hello, Travis," he said, but Travis said nothing in reply. Pete waited for the head of Bentley Brown or Henry Tourville to pop up beside him, but neither of them appeared.

# Chapter
# 30

Rita Peck was getting a little tired of the telephone. It seemed that all she wanted was for the phone to ring, and then the minute it rang, all she wanted was for it to stop. It was never anyone she wanted to talk to anyway. She had collected the usual assortment of calls this afternoon: Sarah Abrew wanted Pete to stop off for some horehound drops on his way over in the morning. Henry's mother wanted to know if Henry had shown up. Ree Brown wanted to know if Carlisle had shown up. Bert Barker wanted a free paint job on his barn, insisting that the one Factotum did for him twelve years ago was faulty since it was now starting to peel. Jean at the police station wanted Pete to take her two nephews, who were visiting from Oklahoma, on a dune buggy ride. Henry's mother wanted Henry again. Ree Brown wanted Pete, although she pretended she wanted Carlisle again. And Rita wanted her daughter, Maxine, to come down the road so she could give her a good smack.

But she absolutely *refused* to worry about her. She thought of all the occasions she had worried about her and worried about her and all the time she was just off acting up somewhere. There was a day when Rita would have let herself get really worked up over this, would even have called the police by now, and all the time Maxine would have been eating french fries at the Shack. She was not going to worry—it was as simple as that.

The phone rang.

"Factotum!" she snapped.

"Rita, honey, listen, it's Bert. How about this, how about we go fifty-fifty? I buy the paint, Pete does the painting. How about that?"

Rita hung up on Bert, something she had never done in her *life,* and dialed the police station. "Chief McOwat please," she said to Jean.

"Not here. That you, Rita? Thought so. He's in Bradford at the hospital picking up some medical records. Something to do with Bentley Brown, but don't tell anyone I told you. He's crabby as an old coot, too, not much like him. Right after Marty Sunderland stopped by, he starts in phoning, phoning, phoning, hollering out the door Jean this, Jean that, then off he tears to Bradford. Now, what can I do for you?"

"Nothing," said Rita. Bentley Brown. One overdue teen-age daughter was not something with which to bother a man who was working on a murder, after all. She thanked Jean and hung up the phone.

# Chapter
# 31

Pete shifted his weight away from the welcome support of the stone wall, foundered in the chest-deep water, and grabbed Maxine's ledge to keep himself afloat. He gave Max's shoulder a squeeze of encouragement. She was shaking again as she stared up at Travis from her perch on the ledge where Connie still clung, as much to keep herself above the water as to warm and comfort the girl, Pete knew. Time. They had very little. Pete had to do something, and he had it in mind to try a false heartiness on the boy overhead, to begin by pretending that Maxine had told them nothing, to thank him for coming to help, to see which way he ran with it.

"Thank God you're here," Pete began, dismayed at the weakness, the lack of carry, in his own voice. He cleared his throat and tried again. "We need some help and we need it fast. I'm not even sure there's enough time for you to go get help and come back. Is there anything up there that would serve as a—"

"We know you killed Bentley," Connie shouted up at him, and Pete closed his eyes and groaned. "What! What? Are you going to pussyfoot around about this all day? You think he's stupid?"

"Zip it," Pete snapped, somewhat surprised to find that

new understanding had done little to dent the old anger, and Connie, ever quick to pick up on a nuance, responded at once and in kind.

"We'd be out of here now if you'd have boosted me up like I told you; now we have to rely on a—"

"We wouldn't have been here at all if you hadn't jumped in this stupid hole in the first place! We wouldn't have been in these *woods* at all if you hadn't insisted that Henry Tourville didn't—"

"Right! Let's count all my mistakes, let's never forget a single one! But you don't have any to count, do you? Not you, not Mr.—"

"I should have tossed you up, all right? I should have rented a room at the Whiteaker so you and Glen could go at it in peace!" Pete stopped, horrified, as his ugly sounds echoed around the cave. Was there some rule about anger, that the longer it was denied, the stronger was its dose? He looked up. Above them, dark eyes blinked in a pale face.

"Travis," said Pete, "what we do or don't know about you and Carlisle is not the big issue at the moment. Whether or not you killed Carlisle doesn't matter right now, it's not the—"

"Carlisle?" Travis Dearborn shot up onto his feet and looked around behind him.

"He means Bentley," said Connie. "Now, get your ass in gear and do something about getting us out."

"Maxine," said Travis. "Is she—"

"She's okay." Pete looked at her crumpled form and hoped she was. "But, I repeat, we don't have a lot of time."

"She was going to turn me in. She saw me, she heard me stealing Henry's ring. When she fell—"

"That's all forgotten now, Travis, but you can't leave her here to die. Now, do you see anything up there that would help us?"

As Pete spoke, Travis Dearborn continued to look around him wildly, but when he looked back down into the cave, it didn't seem that it was *their* skins that were foremost in his mind.

"I didn't do it on purpose. I tell you, it was an accident. I don't deserve to go to jail for this, I tell you, I don't! All I wanted was *her*. I tried to tell her! She wasn't going to have anything more to do with me! I didn't know about him, I didn't know about the baby, she didn't tell me! She just said she wasn't going to see me again, not like that! I couldn't understand it! We loved each other! She told me that's why she did it, because she had loved me for a long time."

"It's okay, Travis," said Pete, trying to keep everything in his voice focused, carrying no note of blame, trying to get Travis past the saving of his own hide and get him to work saving theirs. "None of that matters anymore. If you could—"

"None of that matters anymore! What are you, nuts?" yelled Connie.

Pete whirled around, thinking that in one more minute he really might just kill Connie. She continued to shout up at Travis.

"You're going to jail, Trav, old boy. Let's face facts here. Let's not deal in fantasy, all right? You're going to jail. You've killed one person, accidentally or not—"

"It was. I tell you, it was. We were lying in the sand. She said it was over. She wouldn't listen to me! She wouldn't see reason! She thought if she didn't see me, I'd go back with her sister and it would all be the way it was before, but I told her no, I wouldn't. I told her I wouldn't take no for an answer, and I grabbed her by the shoulders and shook her. I just kept shaking her. I think I was banging her into the sand, I didn't know it, I swear to you I didn't know it! I just kept shaking her, yelling at her, she wouldn't answer me! Then her eyes . . . her eyes . . ." Travis whirled away from the edge of the hole, and Pete couldn't see him anymore. Had he gone? Impossible. He would have to either help them or finish them; he couldn't risk leaving them for someone else to find, it was as simple as that.

"It was an accident," Pete called out. "I can understand that. I can talk to the chief, I can help you explain it."

"*That* was an accident. This won't be. Do you read me up there?"

It seemed unbelievable to Pete that it was Connie's voice, cutting up through the wet, cold air, that finally brought Travis back to the edge of the hole.

"It *was*. It was an accident. There was a flat rock, a huge thing, just under the sand where her head fell, I kept smashing her into it, I didn't *know* it was there! Then all of a sudden her eyes went funny, she was gone, she was—"

"Dead. That's one down and three to go, old boy. Now, I advise you to get your butt in gear up there. Maxine's eyes aren't looking any too swift here either!"

There was no sound from above, no sight of Travis. Pete stared through the darkening murk at Connie. She stared back, chin stretched high, struggling to stay above the rising tide. "You're wrong, you know," she said. "He's no little kid. He's not going to fall for that everything-will-be-forgotten-as-long-as-you-help-us-out line of crap."

Pete didn't answer. He waited. There was no sound from above.

"You should have boosted me up. You should at least have discussed it with me."

"*Discussed* it! You threatened to kill me, you call that a discussion?" He was still yelling, but it was with effort that he did so, and when Connie spoke again, it was soft enough so that he wasn't sure at first that he had heard her right.

"You should have told me you were afraid."

Pete looked at her. The water was licking her neck as well as the ledge, and he suspected that she was hanging from the ledge with her feet off the ground, treading water now. How long could she do that? Was it, after all, going to end right here, like this? Suddenly all his anger left him, to be replaced by a new—or was it old?—emotion. He struggled to maneuver in the water until he was close enough to Connie to touch her. He reached out and laid the cold fingers of his better hand on her equally cold face. She pressed her face into his hand. He raised his other one and held her face between broken plaster on one side and bloody abrasions on the other.

"I'm sorry," she said. "Oh God, I'm so sorry."

"Hey," said a voice from up above, and together they looked up to see Travis once again.

# Chapter
## 32

It was dark, or near enough, and Rita was still resisting the urge to launch a massive search for her daughter when the police chief came walking through the doorway.

He had an air of coincidentally having stopped by, but he asked too many questions, and Rita wasn't fooled for a minute. It was about Bentley; it had to be.

"I was looking for Carlisle Brown. Is she still here, by any chance?"

"I'm sorry, she didn't come in today at all," said Rita. "Her mother was looking for her, too."

The chief looked around the little room and then back at Rita. He smiled with the corner of his mouth and one eye, making it look almost like a wink. "Probably took off with her boyfriend someplace? You haven't see him, either?"

"I believe she and Travis have broken up," said Rita. "I haven't seen him around here in quite some time."

"You haven't. Haven't seen him today, then."

"No." He seemed too interested in Travis. There was something about his squint. Rita considered telling him that Travis Dearborn was seen entering the school woods with Maxine in tow, but she was feeling more and more foolish over her worries and fears about her daughter. She and Maxine had spent a whole summer of tug-of-war over rules and deadlines and curfews, and today was just another in a long line of more of the same. And after all, one didn't admit right off the top of one's head that one suspected one's own daughter of making a fool of herself traipsing through the woods after the most popular boy in the whole school.

"Henry Tourville, he didn't show up here either?"

"No," said Rita. Was it Henry he was interested in? She was more than ever sure now this was all about Bentley. Henry didn't show here, he didn't show for his lab test . . .

"Well!" The chief straightened out his back and stretched his arms. "If you see or hear from any of them, let me know, will you?"

"Certainly," said Rita.

She studied the door in puzzlement after he left. *Any* of them?

# Chapter
33

Maxine was now unconscious. Connie didn't seem to have any qualms about telling Travis this either. She was clinging half to Pete and half to the ledge, coughing out water with every third breath, and still she managed to holler.

"Okay, Travis, this is it! Maxine is out cold. It's now or never, buddy. It's so damned cold in here that she won't live long this way, do you hear me? Do you want to add another to your list?"

"Travis," said Pete. "What happened to Carlisle on the beach was an accident."

"Carlisle? You keep saying Carlisle. It was *Bentley* that I killed. Oh God, it was Bentley I killed." He was crying.

Pete was confused. It was *Carlisle* he killed!

"She did it for a joke. It all started as a joke. Carlisle set her up, set me up, thought it would be funny if they could fool me. What Carlisle didn't know—or did she? maybe she *did* know—but Bentley loved me! She wanted to be with me, to see for herself, to be with *me*."

"Travis," Pete began, but Connie shushed him.

"Carlisle brought it on herself! Oh, I figured out it was Bentley fast enough, and I started to get mad, and then I decided to make a joke on them. I started fooling around with Bentley, see, and then, well, Bentley got upset, scared, so I quit it. And then she told me, and . . . we . . . I don't know, we just started . . . talking, sort of. And I had a good time. Bentley was . . . different. She knew things. And then I started joking around, saying I knew that she wanted to steal me away from Carlisle all along and that's why she played the trick and she got all red, she tried to leave. *She* loved me!''

*She loved me. Was* love everything?

"Carlisle thought I never knew it was Bentley, I told Bentley not to tell her. And then Carlisle wanted to do it again, and I told Bentley to do it, to go ahead, to make the joke on Carlisle, see. I wanted to see *Bentley!* She did it once more, but not again after that, she wouldn't again after that. So then I'd go over at times when I knew Carlisle was out, and I'd get Bentley to walk the beach and meet me sometimes. It was kind of funny, people would see us on the beach from a distance and they'd figure it was me and Carlisle, they just never believed it would be *Bentley!* Not with me. It was kind of funny, I thought, but Bentley, she didn't like it. She started getting scared. Then after . . . then after she finally did it with me, she wouldn't come see me anymore! I made her, finally I made her, I told her I was going to tell Carlisle everything if she didn't come, so she came, that day on the beach. She told me then that it was over. 'Joke's over,' she said. She pretended that was all it was, but I knew it wasn't, I knew how she really loved me! I didn't know about Henry until all of a sudden it was all over the school that he got her pregnant. When I found out, I wanted to kill him. I wanted to kill him! That day after I heard about Henry, when I saw him on the beach with Carlisle, I just thought about how it was his baby and about how he was having her all the time I couldn't, and I wanted to *kill* him! I hit him—''

"I'm afraid there was nothing to know about Henry,'' said a voice from the darkness, and Henry Tourville's head appeared at the edge of the hole, a dark silhouette against their little piece of less sky.

"There was never anything between Bentley and I, and

I'm still not quite sure how a rumor of this nature was born.''

Pete, from down in the freezing water, remembered his conversation with Ree about the Coke-bottle lenses, remembered what he had later said to Connie and why he had said it, and he felt the need to make his own confession. ''I'm afraid I might have been responsible for that particular rumor,'' he interjected, and the sound of his voice seemed to bring at least one of the players above them back into the game they were struggling with down below.

''Well,'' said Henry, and that seemed to be the only word he planned to expend on the subject. ''Now, I think at present the first priority is to get little Max out of this hole, wouldn't you agree?''

''Yes!'' Connie hollered, but Travis was still somewhere else.

''Then who was it?'' he shouted. ''Who was the baby's—''

''Oh, for God's sake!'' said Connie. ''You were. You said so yourself. You said she finally did it with you.''

Pete could actually hear the light dawning in Travis's voice. ''But it was only that once!''

''Oh, for God's sake,'' said Connie. She coughed, and for some reason, she looked hard at Pete.

*Only that once.*

Pete didn't bother to add anything more. Connie had been right, about many things, he was now discovering. He had been wrong about many others. He had looked only as far as the surfaces, he had believed what he had wanted to believe: that there was a right one, and a wrong one. Then he had shut the rest out. He had shut *her* out.

Noise erupted up above around the hole. Henry, who had apparently not been idle in his absence, was lowering some thick rope that had been threaded through what looked like the canvas cover to a deck chair down the shaft and into the cave.

''I'm afraid I have a crime of my own to confess. I broke into the school building and took a few items that I thought might aid in Maxine's exit. I think Travis and I between us could pull her up if you could situate her securely somehow?"

Pete grabbed the contraption when it swung within reach, and Connie positioned it while Pete eased Maxine first into the water and from there into the makeshift sling. It was slow work, made all the slower by the fact that Connie's strength was much diminished, and Pete's hands responded with nothing but pain to his commands. Finally Maxine was pulled up, then Connie, and lastly, Pete, and neither Pete nor Connie would have made that final heave over the edge of the hole onto solid ground if Travis and Henry hadn't been there to muscle them through it. And it was Travis and Henry who carried Maxine between them on the blanket Henry had brought from the school, with Connie and Pete flanking and protecting her from the briars and branches. It was a long hike back through the woods, a trip made all the longer by Travis's continued broken confession, but made more bearable by Henry Tourville's steady presence at Maxine's feet.

"Carlisle knew something was wrong," said Travis, "but I wanted her to stay with me. I was afraid if we broke up, it would call attention to myself, I would become a suspect. I had already done too much. On the beach, when I was shaking her, when Bentley—"

Henry chimed in. "I think we know the rest, old fellow."

"No! No. Let me tell it. I was shaking her. Smashing her into the sand, into that rock, killing her, she knew I was killing her all the time, but I didn't! And she raked at my fingers, clawed at me. She didn't have a chance. I killed her. But my ring came off. At least I think that's how it came off. I dragged her into the water, I wanted her to wash out to sea, I wanted them never to find her! I didn't know until I was at Marty's house. I was at his house and I realized I didn't have my ring. Then Marty had to answer the phone, and I charged around his room scared, oh man, I was so scared! And right there in this glass on his bureau I saw it! I saw his ring! Sitting in the bottom of this glass with all these rubber bands and paper clips and junk like that on top of it, I knew he'd never miss it. I took it. I shoved it in my pocket. And then later I realized it was the wrong year, I stole a ring with the wrong year on it! Oh God, I am so dumb! So the next day in school Alan left his ring on the sink and it was so easy, so easy to pick it up and shove it in my pocket, never thinking that it wasn't going to fit! It was too small! I didn't plan to take yours, Henry, but you were bigger, and you took it off and left it in your locker every time you went to the gym, and you were hanging around Carlisle, besides. I mean I didn't—''

"Understood," said Henry, which Pete, in the circumstances, thought was pretty damned big of him.

"I couldn't get back to Marty's soon enough, so I dumped his ring on the floor at the supermarket where he worked. I wasn't trying to get anyone in trouble. Then I tossed Alan's down on the floor in history class and . . .''

Travis stopped talking and looked at Connie. "You know about that, I guess." Then he looked down at Maxine. "I did just what Maxine says I did," Travis went on, his voice getting breathless from the exertion of carrying her weight and talking his insides out at the same time. "I jammed open the locker with the screwdriver and took Henry's ring. She was right about that." He stopped talking. Pete turned to hold back a branch and saw that Travis was staring down at Maxine's dead-white face and closed eyes. "But she was wrong to love me."

*Wrong to love me.* Pete looked across Maxine's body at Connie's face, only a pale oval of light against the dark trees. The oval turned away.

"Where *is* Carlisle?" Connie's voice spoke, ghostlike, into the trees.

Travis coughed, a cough that racked his body and Maxine's as well. Her injured arm fell out from under Pete's leather jacket and dangled, and Pete tucked it back in and fastened the jacket around her more securely.

"Carlisle was having a hard time of it," said Travis. "I could hardly stand to be with her. I tried, I tried to help her, but she knew. She knew something. She kept looking at me funny when people would say they saw us someplace that she knew we weren't. She kept talking about Bentley, about how all of a sudden she was interested in fixing herself up, how she was wanting to look . . . different all of a sudden. And after Bentley died, Carlisle kept saying she knew something was wrong, she knew she was seeing someone, and I wouldn't say anything, I didn't tell her. But finally she said she didn't want to see me anymore. I didn't want to see her either, *God*, all I wanted was to never see her again! And she had Henry. Or it seemed like she had you, Henry . . . ?"

It was a question, but at the front of the procession, the tall, dark shape didn't speak.

"But I was afraid. I was afraid if we weren't together, she'd . . . she'd . . . I didn't know what she'd do. Then Henry didn't show up in school today, and Carlisle split, and I figured the two of them had figured out the whole thing, and I got even more scared, I needed to talk to her, I needed to make sure she wouldn't . . . I found her out here and I told her, today in the woods. I figured I might as well."

All of a sudden his voice possessed all the effect of a man who was trying to decide whether or not to go to the prom.

Henry, sounding breathless from his burden, began to speak. "I had become suspicious of Carlisle's situation. She had come to lean on me for some things, she could talk to me about some things. She spoke of her suspicion that Bentley had been seeing someone, and she seemed very bitter; I at first assumed this was merely because her sister hadn't taken her into her confidence. They were ordinarily very close. Then after her sister died, she seemed, frankly, quite afraid. I was very . . . fond of Carlisle." Henry cleared his throat, and looked at Travis. "And after observing certain behaviors on your part, Travis, I, well, I'm afraid I correctly interpreted some, but misinterpreted

205

others. It became clear to me that Carlisle was hiding something, covering something up, and I'm afraid I had begun to suspect that there was some involvement of her own that would not stand the clear light of police inquiry. I thought perhaps Carlisle had stumbled upon her sister as she left you, Travis. I thought perhaps, in a fit of rage or jealousy, she might have accidentally, you understand, done something that . . ." Here Henry stopped, shifted his burden, coughed, and continued on. "After you tipped me to it, Pete, it seemed clear that the less vindication of myself I provided the police, the more I would divert them from Carlisle."

Travis whipped around to look at Pete just then, and Pete felt some explanation of his own behavior was necessary. Unfortunately, he could think of none.

"But where is Carlisle now?" he asked instead.

"She called for help from the school, and is waiting there to guide them to you. I felt it was perhaps necessary to hasten back here with whatever tools I could find."

But Pete looked at Henry's still straight back in front of him. Henry had known about Bentley and Travis? And he had seen Carlisle attempt to strike Travis down, he had seen Travis flail out and send her weapon crashing. If he hadn't appeared just then, if it had been left up to Travis, what would have happened to Carlisle? What would have happened to the three of them in the cave? And conversely, if Pete hadn't called out to warn Travis, what would Carlisle have done to *him* if Henry hadn't appeared? Pete looked down at Maxine's slack face. How many tragedies had Henry prevented that night?

Before them, through the woodbine and the ivy and the scrub pines and bull briars, some distant lights now shone, and it was the sight of help that seemed to sap Pete of his last ounce of strength. Connie, too, who up until that moment had been pushing bravely through the vines, seemed to slump, to lag behind, to slip back from her post at Maxine's side until Pete had lost all sight of her. He left Travis and Henry to push ahead toward the voices and the lights. He found Connie sitting on the ground.

"You know, I don't think if you'd boosted me up, I would have been able to make it after all."

"C'mon," said Pete, kneeling down, finding her, touching cold cloth and colder skin. "You push, I'll pull, we're almost there."

# Chapter
# 34

Maxine lay in her hospital bed in Bradford with her leg in traction. Although she could still feel the pain in what they had told her was a concussed head, a fractured femur, and a sprained wrist, she knew that none of those feelings was as dreaded to her as the horrible chill, the cold whisper, the clinging terror, that stayed with her every time she remembered what it was that she had almost done.

*She had let go.* She had been on the ledge, she had loved him and had almost lied for him, and he had left her there. She had not cared then if she lived, *and she had let go.* Oh God! She tossed her head sideways into the pillow, wanting to feel the headache pain, wanting to feel everything, to hear everything, to smell everything, to see everything, to see them all. Even her mother! It was a funny thing about her mother. Now, just when her mother finally had every reason in the world to be really ripped at her, she didn't seem to want to say anything about what had happened at all! She didn't even get all gaspy and fussy around her; she just sat there very subdued, saying nothing, looking at Maxine and listening to her and making her nervous. It was a funny thing, but after a while Maxine kind of started doing things to try to get her annoying, excitable, smothering old fussbudget mother to come back! "I almost died," she said to her finally, at the end of one long afternoon full of nothing but normal conversation and dullness and . . . and *sensibleness*. Her mother just looked out the window and didn't speak for a long, long time.

But she *had* almost died. She had almost, all on her own, caused her own death by that one moment of not caring, by that one moment of failing to look ahead at whatever might come next, or after, or later. She had let go, and there were already things that had come later, people that had come later, that she trembled to think she might have missed.

The steel gray door swung inward, and there He was again. With a small wooden box this time. He sat down very gently on the side of the bed nearest to the table full of all the other things she had been brought—a Walkman from Pete; a stack of brand-new tapes from this stranger, her mother; a crossword puzzle book from Sarah Abrew; a pile of teen magazines from Connie; a pack of playing cards in a box with the gift card still in it saying, "Merry Christmas to Bert from Maisie," from Bert Barker; and hundreds of cards and sixty pots of flowers from just about everybody else on the island.

"Hi," he said.

"Hi," she said back.

He handed her the box. She opened the lid, and first she smelled the cool smell of cedar, and then she heard the song and then she realized it was a music box. "As Time Goes By." It was as if he *knew*, knew what she had almost done to the rest of all her time. She put the prism he had brought her last time inside the box and closed the lid.

"Thanks."

"You're most welcome." He stood up.

"Henry," she said.

He raised his eyebrows. "Yes, Max?"

"Tell me? Please? Nobody will."

He gazed at her through thick lenses.

"My mother acts like she can't hear me when I bring it up, and Pete keeps saying 'later.' "

Henry looked down at his long fingers and then up again at Maxine. "Well, you should certainly be apprised," he said, and he began. Names and facts and places, things she knew, things Henry knew, things Carlisle and Carlisle's mother and Pete and Connie and Marty all knew, things that were nothing in themselves so much, but when put all together added up to Travis killing Bentley. The final straw was Marty Sunderland at last going to the police with his suspicion that Travis had taken his ring from his room, a ring Marty had never worn since he had returned to his old grade, a ring that had then turned up in the supermarket. The chief had found out about Travis's blood type from the hospital in Bradford, and further tests proved he could be the father of Bentley's child. When Carlisle had called from the school, the police chief had hardly needed to hear her jumbled version of events, of how she had known for so long that something was troubling her sister, how since it was not something Bentley could tell her, it could only be one thing . . .

Or maybe the final straw had been Maxine, and her story about the lockers. But no, the real final straw had been Travis's own confession, Travis, who was now in jail, whose future had been erased because of what he'd done and what he'd done to cover up what he'd done.

And all of them, all of them who'd known something and had said nothing, had almost let the futures of three other people be extinguished in the bottom of a cave.

Futures. After Henry had gone, she took out the music box, and played it one more time.

# Chapter
## 35

Through the front windows of Ree's house Pete could see the warm brown of the cardboard boxes piled up at crazy angles, their flaps open, their insides empty. It was true, then. She was leaving. He didn't want to go inside, didn't want to see the house dismantled and changed. He stopped still in the middle of the walk, and she came out to meet him and sat down on the front step just as she had sat on his own back step not all that many days before. Pete walked up to the steps and sat down beside her. "You're leaving."

She nodded.

"I'm sorry," said Pete. He meant that he was sorry for things he had thought, things he hadn't said, hadn't done, hadn't been and could never be for her, but she took it in its simplest context and responded in kind.

"I'm not sorry. Carlisle needs to be someplace else right now, I need to be someplace else right now. There's nothing to hold us here but a lot of pain."

Was he part of the pain? He wanted desperately to explain some of what had made him distrust her so, had made him behave like such a fool. He wanted her to understand why it was that he had nothing to give her right now. He cleared his throat. "Ree . . ."

211

Light fingers on his arm. "Pete." She looked away, shook her head, looked back at him full in the eyes. "You're a nice guy," she said. "I think I told you that once before, but somehow I don't think you believed it. My daughter has no idea who she is right now; I don't want to see that happen to you."

Pete opened his mouth to speak, but the fingers on his arm dug in, silencing him again.

"She was a fool to leave you. Don't you be one, too, all right?"

Connie. She was talking about Connie.

"Give a listen to your own feelings, Pete."

His feelings. Pete didn't know just what his feelings were, all he knew was that he *did* feel, and that what he was feeling wasn't something he had ever felt before. Sometimes he felt better when he started thinking about the things he and Connie had said in the cave, then he would start to feel worse. But for the first time in over a year he felt that this wasn't the end of it. He had to find out, needed desperately to find out, where all this hard-gained ground had left them. He needed to know more, to hear more, to say more. The question was, did Connie?

"She came back, Pete."

*She came back.* And suddenly Pete felt foolish, doltish, completely thickheaded. Of course! Of course Connie wouldn't have, couldn't have, come back to this isolated, insular place unless she also felt that there were things still left to be said between them. Ree *knew* this. Had everyone else known this all along, everyone but Pete? Pete looked hard at Ree, but as he did so, Ree's eyes slid past his face, settling instead onto something behind him, something that made her smile.

"Do you know, I think you were right about him, I really do. I never in all my days saw anyone take so long to do so little. I think he likes me, I really do!"

Pete turned and peered across Ree's lawn to where Jimmy Solene was now rebuilding her retaining wall. Yes, that was one other thing he needed to do. He strode across the lawn and stopped in front of him.

"Jimmy."

Jimmy Solene kept on working.

"Listen," Pete went on. "I just want you to know that I'm sorry about the other night. I mean that. It won't happen again."

Jimmy straightened up and wiped a grimy hand across his forehead. "You really mean that?"

"I really mean that."

"Well, I'm real glad to hear it," said Jimmy, and he shot his right fist into Pete's stomach, then bent down once more to his work.

Pete bent down too.

# Chapter
# 36

"So that's what happened," said Bert. "Pete finds the young fella, trails him through that stretch of woods to the caves, gets there just in the nick of time with poor Maxine already half beat to death with—"

"She fell through to the caves," said Evan Spender, his eyes focused not on Bert's face but down the road. "Nobody beat her half to death with anything."

"Amounts to the same thing. Don't see why they don't charge him with it anyway. Keep him in there a little longer that way. Don't know why we bother paying all this money for a chief of police if Pete's going to keep doing all his work for him and then he won't even charge anybody with anything."

"Involuntary manslaughter," said Evan, "is something."

Bert Barker snorted. Evan Spender's eyes were still fixed on the distant road.

"And besides, Bert," said Ed Healey, "he got Roy Millis fired from his job. You got to give him credit there. A teacher fooling around with the kids . . ."

Bert snorted again. "Natalie Price doesn't look like a kid to me. And what about that time she got caught in the caves with Nat Weams?"

"Nat Weams is a sight nearer her age," said Ed. "Nat Weams isn't her teacher."

"Well, that wasn't Willy's doing either," said Bert. "Connie caught Millis; leastwise, she's the one tipped the chief off to go following him around a bit."

Suddenly Evan Spender got up off the bench in front of Beston's and strolled down the steps and into the street.

"Now what the hell's eating you?" hollered Bert, but Evan didn't answer. He walked down the street until he came up to the steps in front of the post office, where Rita Peck was sitting sorting through her mail.

Ed and Bert watched him bend down and speak to her, then fold himself onto the steps beside her and speak some more, then listen, and listen some more. Rita's hands began to flail left and right, her gleaming black head began to bob, her shoulders rose and fell. She touched her wrist, then lifted her thigh and pointed to it, then raised up an arm and cupped the back of her head.

"Talking about Maxine," Ed reported.

"Hmp," said Bert.

After a while Rita seemed to wind down. Only after she'd remained slumped and quiet for a minute or two did Evan rise from the post office steps and beckon to her. Rita rose with him, and they set off down the street side by side. After a few paces Evan's hand came to rest on the small of her back.

"Nice ass," said Bert.

"Speaking of which," said Ed, "I wish to hell Pete would get off of his and do something about Connie. What's he think she came back for, anyway?"

"Hell," said Bert. "Least he could do is *hire* her again; I been waiting all fall for someone to put up my storm windows. Either that or stop traipsing around in the woods after killers and start concentrating on something important!"

"Like your windows, Bert?"

"Yeah, like my windows," said Bert.

# About the Author

*Sally Gunning* lives on Cape Cod and is hard at work on her next Peter Bartholomew mystery.